"You're avoiding me, Grace, and I want to know why."

Demetrius continued insistently. "You've refused more dates than you've accepted from me. I think you're afraid to acknowledge what's happening between us."

"I swear I don't know what you're talking about!" Grace blurted out in confusion and shock. "To start with, what have I got to be afraid of?"

"You tell me," he said evenly, his eyes not leaving hers. "Being hurt? Commitment? Another affair that might turn sour."

Another affair? She had never had another affair. "My God!" Grace retorted angrily. "You really do take a lot for granted! If you have in mind an affair—"

"Come on, Grace!" Demetrius interrupted impatiently. "Where else do you think we're heading? Sooner or later you and I are going to make love—and don't bother to deny it."

Claudia Jameson lives in Berkshire, England, with her husband and family. She is an extremely popular author in both the Harlequin Presents and Harlequin Romance series. And no wonder! Her lively dialogue and ingenious plots—with the occasional dash of suspense—make her a favorite with romance readers everywhere.

Books by Claudia Jameson

HARLEQUIN ROMANCE

HARLEQUIN PRESENTS

Don't miss any of our special offers. Write to us at the following address for information on our newest releases.

Harlequin Reader Service
901 Fuhrmann Blvd., P.O. Box 1397, Buffalo, NY 14240
Canadian address: P.O. Box 603,
Fort Erie, Ont. L2A 5X3

Playing Safe
Claudia Jameson

Harlequin Books

TORONTO • NEW YORK • LONDON
AMSTERDAM • PARIS • SYDNEY • HAMBURG
STOCKHOLM • ATHENS • TOKYO • MILAN

Original hardcover edition published in 1988
by Mills & Boon Limited

ISBN 0-373-02936-5

Harlequin Romance first edition October 1988

With many thanks to Julie,
from whom the inspiration came.

CHAPTER ONE

IT SOUNDED like a bargain. It was less than two years old and, according to the advertisement in the local paper, it was in immaculate condition.

Grace Allinson put the newspaper to one side, unconsciously narrowing her eyes as she weighed the pros and cons of buying a second-hand BMW. She, personally, could afford to buy the car; the question was whether she could afford to buy it with the profits from her business—because her private money and the living she made from her business were two totally separate entities in her mind. If she stuck to a down-market car she could buy something new for the same price as the BMW. On the other hand, there was something very attractive about the idea of owning, of having earned for herself, a quality car such as the one being advertised, albeit second-hand.

She turned her attention to her appointments book, to *the* appointments book. She was no longer working alone in the business, she had one full-time employee and a part-timer who came in Mondays, Thursdays and Fridays; today was Friday. Mavis and Jillian were both fully qualified beauty therapists, both competent and extremely pleasant to have around.

Mavis came breezing in then, smiling and shivering in the warmth of the salon as she closed the outer door. 'Gosh, it's freezing out there!'

It was, literally, freezing. Grace looked up with a smile. The Beauty Parlour opened at nine and it was ten minutes to nine now, but she herself was always there by eight-thirty, eight-thirty at the latest. 'I know, the wind's awful, isn't it? If only it would drop. I don't know what's happened this year, but the wind's getting to me far more than anything else.'

It had been incessant. Winter had started in the middle of November, it was now February and still bitterly cold. There had been rain, sleet, hail, snow, fog—the lot. And with it all there had been the wind which seemed to be relentless. Everyone was grumbling, everyone was thinking spring would never come. It was the first topic of conversation from every client—and heaven knew, Grace's clients chatted a lot, about anything and everything. In fact, it had come as a surprise to her in the early days, how much people revealed about themselves and their families, their problems, while undergoing beauty treatment.

Maybe this was because they were relaxed, which was most likely a change for them, relaxed and spending some time and money on themselves. Indulging. Whatever it was, it was a very strict rule with Grace and her staff that nothing, ever, in any way, was passed on from one client to the next. If she or her staff should be pinpointed as a source of gossip, of gossip-*spreading*, the reputation of The Beauty Parlour would go right down the drain. All three of them were professional right down to their fingertips, *especially* their fingertips!

'Grace?' Mavis was looking over her shoulder, eyeing the appointments book. 'Is there something you know that I don't?'

'No, no, just a train of thought.' She glanced up, smiling. Her relationship with her staff was easy and pleasant, and the atmosphere in the salon was one of friendliness. The decor was all pastel colours and luxurious in the extreme, and virtually every customer remarked that merely by stepping on to the premises they felt relaxed.

There was a faint aroma of coffee in the air now. Jillian was in the tiny kitchen; it was her first job of the day to put the coffee on and the percolator would be on the go all day.

'Someone new?' Mavis was pointing to a name against the nine-thirty appointment for the sun-shower. It was Melissa Knight. At ten o'clock she was booked for a bikini-line wax and a half-leg wax.

'Mmm.' Grace knew as much as Mavis did, namely that someone who was coming for that sort of treatment was most likely going on a holiday in the sun. Lucky lady. A holiday abroad in February was a very attractive idea, especially in this awful, abnormally windy February.

Mavis glanced along the page and saw that Melissa Knight's treatment wasn't going to end there. She was also booked for a Cathiodermie, followed by a manicure and pedicure. She was going the whole hog. Mavis was about to remark to her boss that the name didn't ring a bell ... but it did. 'I've heard that name before. Can't remember where.'

'Not here. She's new. She booked with me on the phone last week, said she was new to the area.'

Mavis nodded and moved away. Mrs Wakeham was due any minute; she would spend half an hour on one of the sun-beds before having her facial, during which Mavis would be subjected to the latest news about her poodle—which would be left, at Mrs Wakeham's insistence, in the reception area for over an hour. Well, at least it didn't make a noise!

Grace stayed where she was and picked up the post. Half of it was in brown envelopes. Bills. They would all be put into her handbag and dealt with in her office at home. There wasn't room for an office at the salon, every inch of space here was used to its best advantage—partitioned off, mostly. There was a small sauna, two horizontal sun-beds, one sun-shower which was vertical and reminiscent of an upright coffin—not that she would ever compare it so to a client—the room in which waxing was done, another for G5 rotary massage and Faradic Muscle Toning, Aromatherapy, facials, manicures, pedicures, and three regular shower rooms.

Her business was certainly in the right place. Reading was only a few miles away; it was a big town and it was growing rapidly. Many of her clients lived in Reading, but travelled to the salon here in Wokingham because parking was so much easier. There had been a time, though, during her years of full-time training as a beauty therapist, when Grace had not for one instant thought that the business she would eventually establish would be anywhere near the district in which she had been born and brought up. But it was; Wokingham was just a short drive from her birthplace. She had been born in Doveshill, a dot of an area in Berkshire in the South of England, *Royal* Berkshire, to give it its correct name. Berkshire—Doveshill—Allinson Manor. Allinson Manor was the house in which she had been born, and in which she now lived.

Born with the figurative silver spoon, to a beautiful mother and a clever and wealthy father, Grace's childhood had been idyllic. In fact the whole of her life had been ideal until she had met and fallen in love with the man who had proved to be more interested in money than he had been in her. The bad things in her life, all the changes, had happened within twelve months: the disillusionment, finding out the truth about Raymond Ferris, her anger, her *fury*, at her father... and then her mother's death, and the reconciliation with her father, a reconciliation it had taken Mother's death to bring about...

Well, it had, and after qualifying Grace had moved back in to Allinson Manor to live with her father and her brother. Not that either of them were around much. Her brother was at home only during the holidays, he was a postgraduate student doing scientific research at Cambridge. Her father spent his weekdays in London; it took only an hour or so to get to Westminster from the manor, but Sir Nigel chose to live in London during the week. He would be home today, though, he had called Grace from London last night to tell her he would be driving home this morning.

'We're having guests to dinner,' he'd said. 'Will you be in for the evening, Grace? You'll join us? Dinner will be at eight.'

'Yes. Unless you'd rather——'

'Now don't be silly. I want you to meet this couple, the chap is absolutely first rate. You'll like him.'

'Who are they?'

'Our new neighbours.'

'Oh!' It had taken a moment for her to realise what he meant. Firstly, she had to remind herself that her father was referring to the property next to that of the manor. Well, it was 'next door,' but there were some eighteen acres of land separating the houses, owned between them. Eighteen acres, some of which were woods. Colonel Barrington's place, the *late* Colonel Barrington's place, had been on the market for almost a year. Grace knew it had been sold, but that was all she knew. A few weeks ago she had seen a furniture van turning in to the lane which led to the house.

'How come you know these people?' she had asked her father, not that she got a satisfactory answer.

'Oh, I've known him some years. We've done a spot of business together from time to time.'

It didn't tell her much, not that she was interested. Her father's 'spots of business' did not concern or interest her any more than his politics did. His or anyone else's. It was probably something to do with land, of which he owned quite a lot in Berkshire. He didn't even mention the couple's name, not that that mattered, either, although she had wanted to ask what sort of age group they were in. There hadn't been time. Sir Nigel had rung off after asking her to warn the housekeeper that there would be two extra mouths to feed at dinner on Friday evening.

The bell on the back of the outer door tinkled and Grace looked up to see Mrs Wakeham and her ever-present poodle standing there. They were both covered with snowflakes and, while the poodle was making no protest, it being wrapped in a hand-knitted coat, Mrs Wakeham was making no secret of her feelings about the weather.

'Good heavens, when is it going to let up, Grace? Honestly, I'm seriously considering going to live abroad for the winters. I'm not getting any younger, you know, and I really don't think I can put up with this cold for much longer.'

Grace opened her mouth to commiserate, but she got no further. 'I was saying to Desmond,' her client went on, fluffing the poodle's head, 'that it's high time he retired. Don't you think? He's sixty-seven and really has no need at all to carry on working. I think he likes it,' she added with a certain amount of bewilderment.

Grace smiled, inclining her head in a feminine mannerism of which she was unaware. Her long, elegant hands came up in protest, while her black sheet of shining hair slid across her shoulders. This lady was not merely a client but also a friend, a family friend of long-standing. 'You've been saying that for years, Belle. Of *course* he likes it. He's brilliant, and you know it. Now, what would I do if he weren't there to look after my teeth?'

Belle Wakeham grunted—a very ladylike grunt. She knew full well how good a dentist her husband was, but this girl had been born with perfect teeth. Some would say her teeth were her best asset. She had known Grace Allinson for twenty years, since she was four, and her husband had been taking care of her teeth all that time. She was an attractive child, always had been, and yet she could not be described as beautiful. Attractive but not beautiful, definitely not. Her nose was very straight and in Belle's opinion just a little too long. Her lips were bow-like, but in Belle's opinion just a little too thin. Of course, her eyes were—well, maybe they were *too* large, great big blue eyes. Doe-like. One had to suppose it was an aristocratic face . . . if a little bony. Yes, there was all of that, all those flaws, yet she *was* attractive, very. These days, she certainly knew how to play up the best God had given her and how to play down the worst.

When it came to her brains, however . . . privately, Belle was disappointed that Grace had not ended up at Cambridge like her brother, for she certainly had the brains. This business of hers was surely just a means of keeping herself occupied, although on the other hand, and the girl had to be applauded for this, she really believed in what she was doing. As it happened, so did Belle; she wouldn't be here otherwise. In fact, if one so much as asked a simple question about skin care, nail care, one's hair condition, wrinkled skin or superfluous hair on the chin, Grace would plunge into details so—so *detailed*—one would get quite lost! In other words, she knew her business.

'Humph!' The elderly Belle placed her poodle very carefully on the deep, soft, dusty-pink carpet, tied its lead to a leg of the two-seater cane settee and straightened. 'I'm not sure where that leaves me, my dear. Freezing in this wind. How's your father?'

Grace bit back a smile. Poor Belle, childless and frustrated, wasn't she? Wasn't that poodle a child substitute? She was on every committee, charity fund-raising mainly, within a fifty-mile radius of Reading—and she was a busybody. One could not dislike Belle; basically she was just lonely. She came to The Beauty Parlour mainly because she could natter and have an attentive ear.

'He's fine.' Grace paused, considering whether or not to throw a little food for thought Belle's way. 'In fact ... I'm beginning to think there might be a romance in the air. He hasn't said a word to me, but twice when I've phoned him at his house in London recently, he's had company. Female company.'

She did not get the response she expected. There were no raised eyebrows, no murmurs of approval or disapproval, there was only a little smile—which gave Grace the distinct impression that Belle Wakeham knew something that she did not. It irritated her. It shouldn't have, but it did. *What* was there to know, if anything? Was Belle being deliberately mysterious, or was there something? If there was, why the devil didn't her father say something about it? Was their capacity for communication so limited, so retarded, that he felt he couldn't? Well, if he wasn't going to tell her, she was not going to ask!

'I'd better get on,' the older woman said, meaning get on the sun-bed. Grace let her go without further comment. Belle could have afforded a dozen sun-beds of her own ... which wasn't the point.

Intent on opening the post, Grace picked up the dagger-like letter opener which had been one of many little Christmas presents from her brother—but that was as far as she got. The bell on the outer door tinkled again, the inner door opened and closed quickly, and a white-faced teenager stood in front of the reception desk, looking totally disorientated and extremely upset. Not only was it very obvious that she had been crying, it was also very obvious that she had only just stopped doing so.

The tears on her cheeks were still wet, her mouth was trembling and her eyes were red-rimmed. She looked at Grace and blurted rather than spoke her greeting. 'I—Melissa Knight. I'm sorry I'm early but my brother—er—I'm booked for sun-ray and . . . and everything.'

Grace took one look at her face and felt her heart tug. Lord, the girl was so upset! And she was so pretty! What was she doing here? Of course, one should look after one's skin from an early age, the earlier the better, but not many of her clients were this young. How young? Sixteen? Seventeen? The girl was a doll, an absolute doll. Black-haired, brown-eyed, she was white-skinned, with two perfect rosy cheeks which the warmth of the salon was beginning to restore to their natural colour.

Grace rose from her seat, held out her hand. Every movement was smooth and befitting her name. She had been graceful when she was two years old—not that she knew it. She still had no idea how lovely she was, she knew only that she wished to make the best of herself, and that in her opinion every woman should.

'Miss Knight.' Was it, in fact, *Miss* Knight? The girl's clothes were colourful and ultra-modern, if not to say way-out, and she had rings on every finger except for the pinky on her right hand. Well, there was no contradiction forthcoming, just a somewhat vacant stare which belied the intelligence in the dark, dark eyes. 'I'm Grace Allinson, I own the salon. How do you do?'

No response. Just the same look of bewilderment.

'You said you were new to the area, Miss Knight?'

'Yes, I ... my brother ...'

There it was again. Her brother—what? Grace kept the smile on her face, offering a cup of coffee which was refused, very politely refused.

'No, thank you, I—I'd better—er—I suppose I'll be here all morning, really? I was going to ask if you could do my eyebrows and make-up my face too, but ... it doesn't matter. Demetrius will—well, thank you. Er—where do I go?'

Grace blinked in surprise and covered it by widening her smile. There were a dozen thoughts zipping through her head, and they weren't all of a professional nature. Certainly she wanted to see this young girl relaxed; she was, in fact, itching to get her on the table and tend to her face—which in time she would, because it was she herself who would do the Cathiodermie, a deep-cleansing procedure which was very relaxing. But overriding this was a purely fellow-feeling of sympathy. So dark, tall and slender, the girl was very reminiscent of Grace herself at that age. She led Melissa Knight into the little cubicle where the upright sun-shower was, chattering constantly, deliberately, about goggles and exposure-time and so on, but none of it worked, none of it helped. The girl still looked upset.

'Well, I'll leave you to it, then.' Grace backed away, smiling.

'Thank you, Mrs——'

'Miss.' She repeated her name in full. 'It's Grace Allinson.'

'Allinson!' Melissa Knight looked at her now with a mixture of surprise and chagrin. 'You're not—I mean, are you any relation to Sir Nigel Allinson, the MP?'

'He's my father.' It was a question Grace was used to. Her father knew hundreds of people; maybe this was one of his constituents. 'You've met him?'

'I never dreamt——' The teenager seemed bemused now. 'I mean, that you would...'

'Own a beauty salon?' Grace finished the sentence with a little laugh. She was aware that a lot of people assumed she was merely amusing herself with her beauty business, that it was something she did just to fill her time. 'I know, it isn't quite the thing people expect Sir Nigel Allinson's daughter to do.'

'Oh! But I didn't mean... I mean, I think it's marvellous, honestly. I think you're lucky to have your own business!'

Inwardly, Grace was laughing again. Lucky? While she counted herself fortunate in many respects, her having a successful business was not attributable to good luck. So-called good luck was something she did not believe in. She had planned and schemed carefully, had chosen her co-workers carefully and she had worked damned hard to get where she was.

No, it was good management, not good luck. If she had taken advantage of the 'luck' that was on her side, she would have chosen the easy road rather than the independent one. She would have allowed her father to pave the way for her—to *pay* the way for her. Or she would have approached the people who took care of, controlled for her, the money left to her by her mother and her grandparents, money which would be under her own control by the end of the year, when she was twenty-five. If her trustees had approved her plans, her private money would have bought her everything she'd needed to start her business. Easy, that would have been. Meaningful, to her, it would not. It was very important to Grace that she was her own woman. She had had something to prove to herself . . . and to her father. Oh, she and he were friends these days—on the surface—they even lived together, but she would never forget her humiliation, would never forget the way *he* had humiliated her five years ago, when she had been nineteen, when he had bought off her fiancé for thirty pieces of silver. Thirty pieces of silver which her fiancé, Raymond Ferris, had been glad of!

'Have you met my father?' she asked again, seeing the look of curiosity on the younger girl's face.

'No, I haven't—but I'm going to, tonight!' She smiled finally and held out her hand again. 'I'm your new neighbour. Your father has invited me and my brother to dinner at your house tonight.'

'Really?' It was Grace's turn to be surprised. Her father hadn't mentioned that their new neighbours had children—and that they were invited, too. The housekeeper, Matilda, had been told to expect only two people. 'Isn't it a small world? Fancy your coming here when——'

'I know, and I've never been to a beauty salon before.'

'Then you're in for a treat.' Grace was smiling again. She couldn't linger; there was a lot she wanted to ask, but if she didn't let Melissa get on with it, the bookings for the sun-shower would overlap. She did have to clarify things about dinner that night, though, for Matty's benefit. 'My father told me you were coming, but he didn't mention

your name. Yours or your parents', I mean. I hadn't
realised——'

'Oh, there are no parents.' Melissa looked at her
as if she'd said something stupid. 'I'm sorry, I
should explain, you're obviously not in the picture.
My brother has bought the property next to yours.
He's a lot older than I am. Our parents are both
dead.'

'Oh! I see. So it will be just the two of you
tonight?'

'Yes.' She seemed to relax suddenly. 'And that's
why I've come here. I've been working hard in the
house, the sauna and the pool aren't finished yet
and I—well, I felt I needed to do something to pick
myself up, if you see what I mean. I feel wrinkled
and grubby and exhausted.'

Grace couldn't help laughing. She had liked this
girl at once, quite apart from feeling sorry for her,
which she still did. She was looking at Grace with
those huge dark eyes, saying what a physical wreck
she felt. 'If it's any consolation, Melissa—may I
call you Melissa?—you don't look it! You'll feel on
top of the world by the time you leave here.'

'I have to be ready to leave by one.' The words
were blurted, a worried look creeping into her eyes.
'Demetrius is picking me up, and he won't be
pleased if I'm not ready.'

'Demetrius? Your brother?' Was it he who had
been responsible for her tears earlier? She sounded
as though she was frightened of him.

There was a swift nod. 'We're half-Greek, you
know.'

Grace giggled at that. 'No, I didn't know.' She
glanced at her watch. 'You must press on. We can
chat while I'm ministering to you later.' A thought

struck her. 'Look, if you'd like to have an ordinary facial instead of the Cathiodermie, we'll save about half an hour and I'll have time to pluck your eyebrows and make-up your face. How does that sound?'

It was agreed. When Grace took over with her an hour or so later, she was more relaxed—though lamenting her decision to have her legs and bikini-line waxed. 'It hurt! Oh, that's no reflection on your assistant—Mavis, isn't it? She did it as swiftly as she could, but I've never had that done before, so I just thought I'd try it while I was here, but I don't think I'll bother again!'

'It gets better,' Grace promised. 'The hair grows back weaker, you know. And what's all this for? Are you planning a holiday in the sun now you're settled in?'

'We're nowhere near settled in yet! No, I can't go on holiday. Demetrius won't allow it. He's confiscated my passport.'

Grace stared at her. 'Confiscated . . . ? But why on earth should he do such a thing?' She regretted the question as soon as it was out, it really was none of her business. But Melissa didn't seem to mind; on the contrary, she talked so much during the following hour and a half that Grace had the impression there was no one else she could talk to. It was an accurate impression.

'You needn't sound so shocked, my brother is capable of far worse than that! At least, as far as I'm concerned. I can't get away with *anything*,' she added dramatically. 'He's hidden my passport because he thinks I might take off for Athens at any moment.'

Grace was staring at her again. It went unnoticed because Melissa's eyes were closed. 'Athens? Why Athens?'

There was a delay before she answered that. 'We have a house there,' she said finally, her voice matter of fact. Then, opening her eyes to glance up at Grace, 'Well, to be honest I have—or rather I had—a boyfriend there. Someone my brother disapproves of.'

'I see.'

'You couldn't possibly see,' Melissa told her firmly. 'I mean Demetrius has forbidden me ever to see him again. What I'm trying to tell you is that my brother doesn't know when to mind his own business.'

Grace smiled; the story was all too familiar. 'Believe it or not, I do know the feeling. Something similar happened to me once.'

'Your brother interfered in your life?'

'No, my father did. But it all came right in the end.' It was the truth. Grace had not forgotten, but she had forgiven her father for interfering in her life. She had learned from the past; it had changed her, inevitably, irrevocably, but she had to admit she had changed for the better.

At first she had been bitter—then the bitterness became determination. After her experience with Raymond, concluding with that awful episode with her father, she had set out to prove that she was not the idiot everyone seemed to think she was. The moment she had qualified and left college, she had approached not her trustees but the local bank. She had got a loan for her business on the strength of her own personality and plans, not on the strength of her family's wealth or her father's title or standing in the community.

Her father had praised her for her efforts. Only a few weeks ago he had tipped an imaginary hat while they'd been dining, and had said, 'I take my hat off to you, Grace, you've done very well.'

It had been high praise indeed, coming from him. She had had something to prove to him and she had succeeded. Her business was flourishing and Sir Nigel Allinson had had not the slightest influence on that; she had achieved it solely through her own efforts, and to describe that as satisfying would be an understatement.

'You're not going to tell me,' Melissa was saying, 'that my brother was acting in my best interests?'

Grace noted the cynicism and answered diplomatically. How else could she comment? She didn't know the circumstances and she didn't know Demetrius Knight. 'I'm sure he believed he was.'

Melissa snorted. 'I can't see that at all. Just wait till you meet him, you'll see how bossy he is. I mean, I didn't want to come and live in the country, you know. It was *his* idea.'

'He wanted a house in the country, did he?'

There was hesitation. 'So he said. I suppose— well, he moved his head offices recently. To Bracknell. So I suppose it will be handy for him, but it's all right for him, he's still got the apartment overlooking Hyde Park. I loved it there.'

Grace was intrigued. 'His head offices? What type of business is he in?'

'Ha! You name it. He has a building company, he owns property all over the show, he has shares in racehorses, he plays the stock-market, his latest acquisition is a factory which manufactures surgical instruments, he—shall I go on?'

The older girl was laughing, shaking her head. 'Don't bother, I've got the picture. Perhaps it would be easier if you just described your brother as an entrepreneur.'

'He's more than that.' But there was no pride in Melissa's voice, there was resentment. It was unmistakable. 'Demetrius has the Midas touch, he can take over an ailing business and make it into a gold mine.'

'And don't you think that's admirable?' Grace probed.

There was a grunt, no direct answer. Melissa reverted to her previous theme. 'I don't think I'm going to like living in the country. I already miss London. It's so—so *lively*.'

'But it's only an hour away, straight down the M4! What's the problem? Or can't you drive—are you actually old enough to drive?'

There was laughter at that. 'I'm eighteen, but thanks for the compliment. I passed my driving test when I was seventeen, but I lost my licence last month.' She opened one eye and peered up at Grace, keen to see her reaction. Grace didn't react until she added, 'For a year, for drinking and driving. I got caught speeding.'

'Wow!'

'I know.' The brown eyes closed again. 'I thought Demetrius would kill me, he very nearly did. He still isn't over it yet, he's making me sell my car. He gave it to me when I passed my test and told me I had to be responsible for it. Now he's forbidden me to hang on to it and he says I have to be responsible for selling it myself. He's always going on about responsibility. Of course it would just depreciate, standing there unused. You don't know anyone who wants to buy a secondhand BMW do you?'

'I don't believe this...it isn't red, by any chance?'

It was. It was the one advertised in the local paper; Melissa had put the ad in only the day before. By the time one o'clock rolled around, the two of them were friends and Grace was almost ready to buy the car sight unseen. She was also thoroughly sick of hearing the name Demetrius. If Melissa mentioned him once, she mentioned him a hundred times. Even allowing for her dramatic way of speaking, one had the feeling that she really couldn't draw breath without getting her brother's permission first. Grace privately admitted that he sounded like the archetypal male chauvinist pig. A Greek one, or half-Greek one, at that. She had given Melissa no hint of it, but she was not exactly looking forward to having him at the manor for dinner that evening. She disliked the man even before setting eyes on him. When she did set eyes on him, it got worse.

He didn't come in to the salon to collect his sister, not at first. The first sign of his being in the vicinity was the impatient tooting of a car horn outside the front door. There were double yellow lines right outside, but there were parking spaces at the side of the building, two of which were private and reserved for the salon's clients.

Grace was sitting in reception, having handed Melissa over to Mavis for her manicure and pedicure. She glanced outside when she heard the tooting, caught a glimpse of a silver-coloured car and thought no more of it. Half a minute later it started again. Again she ignored it. Then the door was flung open and Demetrius Knight stepped inside, looking as if he was ready to tear the place to pieces. There was no mistaking who he was, he was as darkly handsome as his sister was beautiful. Their resemblance was striking, although he had quite a different skin tone and none of her apparent physical frailty. He was tall and broad and as solid as a rock, his shoulders seeming massive in the immaculate black overcoat he was wearing. He was also a great deal older than Melissa. In fact, he could have been twice her age.

He glanced around with a look of open distaste, let his eyes come to rest on Grace and, with a face like thunder, stood towering over her, his open palm slamming against the reception counter.

'My name is Knight. I believe you have my sister in here,' he barked, as if they were keeping Melissa in captivity. 'Kindly inform her that it is now one o'clock precisely and that I am parked on yellow lines. In other words, tell her to get a move on.'

Grace almost laughed aloud. Her impressions of this man had been very accurate indeed. He was the ultimate autocrat. 'Ah, yes,' she said smoothly, getting to her feet, 'your sister won't be long, Mr Knight. May I suggest you put your car at the side of the building for a few minutes? There are parking spaces——'

He wasn't even looking at her now, he was looking at his watch. 'One minute past. Fetch her. Now. There's a good girl.'

It had been a long, long time since Grace had gone red in the face; she wasn't given to blushing and these days she wasn't given to spasms of temper. She experienced both in that instant. Anger shot through her, bringing a red flush to her cheeks. How dared he talk to her like that, as though she was an office junior? 'I'll see how she's doing,' she said stiffly, her eyes flitting to the door leading to the rear of the salon. 'Only she's having a manicure now and——'

'My dear girl,' he interrupted impatiently, 'I don't care if she's in the throes of having her head shaved. We have a luncheon appointment and I want her out here now. Do you understand me?'

Grace pulled herself to her full height, which was a good five feet eight, and looked directly at him. 'Yes, Mr Knight,' she said, with as much sarcasm as she could muster, 'unfortunately I think I do.'

CHAPTER TWO

'OBNOXIOUS? What on earth do you mean, Grace?'
Sir Nigel Allinson peered at his daughter over the
horn-rimmed bifocals he had been wearing for
years, his bushy eyebrows drawn together. He was
dressed in one of the brown pin-stripe suits he
favoured, and she observed that he'd put on some
weight lately. He was also going rapidly grey where
he wasn't bald. It was unfortunate because it made
him look older than his years; he was fifty-five but
he looked sixty-five.

'You heard me, Daddy. I chose the word with
care. I disliked the man before I even set eyes on
him.'

'Which was ridiculous of you.' Grace's father
didn't seem to be taking her seriously. She had been
home from work five minutes and had been talking
about Melissa and Demetrius Knight. 'Ah, here's
our tea...'

Matilda came in with a tray, placed it carefully
on a side table near the sofa Grace was occupying
and, with a quick wink at her, retreated.

'Thank you, Matty.' Grace smiled fondly at the
housekeeper. She had been in her father's employ
since before Grace was born, before her brother
Thomas was born, actually, and she was, if not
quite like a member of the family, a friend and
comfort to have around. She was grey-haired, sixty,
stocky and extremely efficient and hardworking.

'Not at all,' Grace continued as she poured the tea. 'Granted, I don't know the family's circumstances, but it was obvious to me that Demetrius Knight is a bully.'

'A bully? My dear child, that young man has come from nothing, he's achieved more in——'

'In what way is that relevant?'

Sir Nigel let his impatience be known. 'You're being emotional. Of course it's relevant. He is ruthless in business, but what I'm trying to tell you is that he cares very much about that sister of his—and she's a headache to him.'

'She told me you haven't met her.'

'I haven't.' He took the point, inclining his head. 'But, unlike you, I'm entitled to pre-judge.'

'Oh, really? How come?'

'I'm in command of the facts—I happen to know that the girl is wild. She's been on her brother's hands since she left boarding-school last summer, and I'm sure he's at his wits' end. He doesn't know what to do with her. She's irresponsible and running wild—or she would be, if he left her to her own devices.'

'And what is he doing instead? He's forcing her to live out here, from what I can gather. She doesn't want to live in the country.'

Sir Nigel had had enough. He picked up the *Financial Times*, effectively telling his daughter he didn't want to hear any more. Grace's glare went unnoticed. It was no use being irritated with her father when it was Demetrius Knight she was irritated with. She was not looking forward to spending an evening with him, she hadn't got over the way he had spoken to her earlier in the day.

Melissa had emerged from her treatment, taken one look at his face and left the salon looking just as tense as she had when she'd entered it. There had been no time for introductions; he had barely allowed his sister time to write a cheque before whisking her away. The only pleasant moment had been when he'd first set eyes on Melissa, and his face had registered momentary surprise at her appearance. The make-up job Grace had done on her had been superb; it was subtle and flattering, bringing out the best in the young woman's features—not that that had been difficult.

Demetrius Knight had been momentarily taken aback, had blinked and muttered something about her looking grown-up. Grace had turned away at that point, not wishing to show her annoyance. Grown-up? Melissa *was* grown-up, she was eighteen. Oh, she seemed younger than her years in some respects, but she was hardly the child he treated her as, and Grace did not believe she was 'wild', in spite of the loss of her driving licence.

'I'll go and dress,' she told her father. 'What time are we expecting them?'

'Seven for eight, I told you that last night.'

So he had. She sighed inwardly and made her way upstairs. The manor was a large, old house which she loved dearly, every nook and cranny of it. But it was good to have her own rooms, not just a bedroom and bathroom, but her own sitting-room and an office as well. They were decorated and furnished precisely to her taste and were something of a sanctuary to her, especially when her father was in one of his particularly non-communicative moods, like just now. She flipped on a cassette, kicked off her shoes and headed for her bedroom.

She would decide what to wear before she bathed. There was plenty to choose from in her wardrobe, but she wanted something appropriate, something which would be smart but not stuffy.

The telephone rang before she had made a decision. It was Rodney Featherstone, an old friend of her brother's whom she went out with occasionally. She had a date with him for the following evening, he was taking her in to London to see a new musical. Or rather—he should have been.

'You've got to cancel?' She wasn't perturbed, she was sorrier about missing the show than not seeing him.

'Don't sound so upset.' Rodney was laughing at her. 'Anyhow, I'm sorry, Grace, but I have to go to Birmingham for the weekend.'

'Have to, Rodney?' She sank on to the side of her bed, grinning now. 'Who is she?'

'Grace! Would I cancel a date with you for the sake of seeing some other woman?'

'Certainly.' And why shouldn't he? She and he were friends, that was all.

'You wound me. No, it's a party, one I really can't get out of. I'm going with my parents. Somebody's silver wedding.'

She wasn't going to let him off easily. 'That sounds like so much nonsense. Silver weddings are not things which creep up on people, they're planned in advance.'

He was laughing at her again. 'Grace, you are adorable, you know that? I think I love you.'

'Then explain yourself.'

'I was told about it six months ago,' he said, 'and forgot. I didn't put it in my diary because it didn't exactly stick in my mind at the time. But Ma and

Pa will be put out if I let them down, we've all
known these people for yonks.'

'Humph.'

'Grace? Grace!'

'Oh, all right, all right. Have fun. Ring me next
week or whenever.' And with that she hung up,
Rodney being instantly forgotten as she went back
to her wardrobe.

An hour later she was sitting in front of her
dressing-table, putting the finishing touches to her
make-up. She had started from scratch, having
bathed and washed her hair. It hung loosely to her
shoulders, a black sheet moving like silk, shining
as the light caught it. She stood and surveyed herself
in the full-length mirror, aware that she wanted to
make a good impression on Demetrius Knight, and
annoyed with herself for wanting to. It was just that
she wanted to look different, to present a different
image from the woman who had been wearing a
white overall earlier in the day, the woman he had
spoken to as if she were a servant.

Well, she had achieved that. The black cashmere
dress clung lovingly to her figure and looked good
with the silver belt, high-heeled sandals and silver
drop ear-rings. Plain and simple and tasteful, she
looked expensive, sophisticated but not severe.
Giving the impression of severity had been tempting
but not appropriate, considering Melissa, which was
why she had left her hair down.

Moving to the windows which overlooked the
back of the house, she pulled the curtains aside and
looked out. The moon was high and full, the night
windy, the sky as clear as ice. In the distance was
Colonel Barrington's property—the Knights'
property now—but she couldn't actually see it. The

woods obscured the view. Nearer home, shapes she could make out were those of the stables where her yearling, Annabel, was housed, and the paddocks and outhouses. She wondered idly whether Melissa could ride. Perhaps they could go riding together?

Melissa and her brother arrived on the dot of seven, and were shown in to the drawing-room where Grace and her father were waiting. Matilda showed them in; these days she was the only staff who lived in, apart from the gardener who had a small cottage on the edge of the property. The cleaning of the manor was done by a local woman who came in from ten till four on weekdays, and Sir Nigel's chauffeur didn't work at weekends.

Seeing Demetrius Knight again was a shock. It shouldn't have been, but it was. There was no stress, no tension in his features now, his face and his entire body were relaxed as he walked into the drawing-room, and Grace couldn't help noticing that he moved lightly, lithely for a man his size. He was big but not as bulky as she'd imagined, now she saw him without his overcoat. Dressed in a light grey, fine wool suit, a pale blue shirt and contrasting tie, he looked undeniably elegant. His height contributed to that impression, he was a good six inches taller than she, in spite of her heels.

Melissa was hanging back a little, looking uncertain, and it was at her that Grace smiled before turning to her brother. Quite deliberately, she asked Melissa to introduce them.

'There's hardly any need for that,' Demetrius intervened, his voice smooth, his unbelievably dark eyes looking straight into hers. 'We've already met, remember?'

'I remember, Mr Knight.' Grace held out her hand, she was going to have this right and proper whether he liked it or not. 'Grace Allinson...at your service.'

'Good God!' Sir Nigel laughed at her. 'You're being very formal, darling girl!'

But the crack had not gone unappreciated. Demetrius Knight was smiling now...and it was all Grace could do to keep her sudden intake of breath silent. Unlike Melissa, he looked Greek; his skin was olive-coloured, making the contrast of white teeth quite startling. Lights of amusement appeared in the depths of his eyes as he took the proffered hand and bowed—formally, mockingly.

Grace's eyes skimmed involuntarily over the bowed head of hair as black as coal, a riot of curls kept very short in an effort to tame them. For an instant she thought he was going to raise her hand to his lips. She was quite wrong about that. There was nothing flowery about this man, not in any way. One dark eyebrow rose sardonically as he looked down at her. 'How do you do?'

Melissa giggled before another word could be said. 'Demetrius was astonished when I told him who you were earlier.'

'I can imagine.' Grace smiled up at him, her sweetest perfect-hostess smile.

'Naturally, I had no way of knowing.'

'But it shouldn't have made any difference, knowing my name. Still, if you had, I'm sure you wouldn't have been so...brusque?'

The lights in his eyes went out, instantly. Only then did he let go of her hand, releasing it abruptly from his uncomfortably tight grasp. 'Clearly I made a very bad impression.'

Sir Nigel stepped forward. 'And you must be Melissa. I've heard so much about you.' He took the younger girl's hand and shook it. Her eyes flitted firstly to her brother and then to Grace, a faint blush colouring her cheeks.

'Now you've really worried her, Daddy! Come on, Melissa, sit yourself down and tell us what you'd like to drink.'

She asked for a sweet sherry, her brother asked for a Scotch on the rocks. Sir Nigel saw to the drinks while Grace plunged into small talk—it was going to be one of those evenings. She felt she had a lot in common with Melissa, more than the men would realise, but nothing at all with Demetrius.

'Melissa mentioned that you moved your head offices to Bracknell recently, Mr Knight. Does that mean you'll be spending most of your time there?'

Several seconds passed before he answered. It was so long a time, so uncomfortable a time because he did no more than look at her, that Grace began to wonder what she'd said wrong. 'Mr Knight?'

'Not necessarily,' he said finally. 'And the name is Demetrius. I'm sure my sister mentioned also that we're half-Greek.'

'Yes, I—she did.' Grace was ruffled. Somehow he had managed to put her down, at least, that was how she felt. He was sitting several yards from her, yet she could feel the irritation emanating from him. She dragged her eyes from his glare and addressed Melissa. 'On whose side?'

'Our mother's. Our father was English.'

'I'm sure Miss Allinson had gathered that much, Melissa.'

'Grace,' she corrected. 'Please.'

'One waits to be invited,' he told her, inclining his head in acknowledgement. 'Does one not?'

Grace was regretting everything she'd said from the moment he'd walked in. She should not have let her animosity show, clever though she thought she'd been with it. He had picked it up all right, picked it up, added to it, and was throwing it back at her now. She would get no change whatever out of this man. For a moment she was stuck for words.

He spoke next. 'You've lived around here all your life, I take it?'

'Give or take a couple of years. I lived in London when I was training.'

'Training? Ah yes, as a beautician.' There was a small smile, just a slight pause before he said the last word.

'A beauty therapist, if you don't mind.'

'Which implies there's a difference?'

There was a difference: a beautician was concerned mainly with surface appearance, hairdressing, make-up, manicure and so on, while a beauty therapist dealt with much more, with myriad problems, and underwent a very thorough and comprehensive training. 'There is a difference. A beauty——'

'You'll have to explain it to me some time.' He cut her off, turning to accept the drink Sir Nigel was handing him. 'Cheers, Nigel.' He glanced from his host to his hostess, allowing a grin. 'I have to say it came as a surprise today, Nigel, when I learned that your daughter panders to the vanity of women. Tell me, Grace, is it exploitation of the idle, the ugly or the overweight? Or all three?'

Oh, he was clever! Grace was unaware of the way her fingers dug into the arms of her chair. She couldn't believe her ears. He had delivered his questions, his *insults*, smilingly, smoothly, so casually that he had Sir Nigel laughing, oblivious to his sarcasm, his rudeness.

Melissa leapt immediately to Grace's defence, but the older girl held up a hand. 'Oh, don't worry about that. In their ignorance, lots of men make such silly remarks. If you'll excuse me a moment, I'll see how dinner's progressing.'

Out, she had to get out of the room for a moment. She was fuming. She went into the kitchen, closed the door behind her and just stood there, breathing deeply.

'Miss Gracie?' Matilda threw her a look of concern, reverting to the name they had called her as a child. 'Are you all right?'

'Yes, of course, Matty. I—I don't think our new neighbours are going to be the easiest people to entertain,' she added lightly.

'Our new neighbours? Is that who they are? I thought they were people Sir Nigel knew from London.'

'They are. Well, the gentleman is.' Gentleman? The word almost stuck in her throat.

'And they're the ones who've bought the Colonel's house? I know there's been a lot of alterations going on over there.'

'You know more than I do.'

'Oh, yes, I hear they've been knocking walls down and all sorts of things. They're having a swimming pool put in, too.'

It was always like that with Matty. Where she got her information was a mystery. 'Mmm.' Grace turned to leave.

'But—did you want something?' The housekeeper was at a loss. 'I mean, did you want to ask
me something?'

'No, Matty. I just came in for a breather.'

She rejoined her guests in the drawing-room,
composed again.

Towards the end of dinner Sir Nigel and
Demetrius slipped into business talk, about stocks
and shares and some company which had just gone
bust. Such talk was inevitable, Grace supposed, and
as soon as they'd finished eating she suggested that
she and Melissa left them to it. 'I'm going to show
Melissa around the house, Daddy. We'll join you
and Demetrius shortly for coffee.'

They hardly acknowledged her. She turned to
Melissa. 'Would you like me to show you around?'

The girl was obviously relieved and not merely
being polite, for her eyes lit up. 'I'd love it. I was
admiring that panelling in the hall and—have you
got a library?'

'You bet.' Grace was amused, but Melissa's
interest in the house was genuine. She asked questions about its history and she made intelligent remarks about the place, going on to say what she
had planned for her own new home.

'Demetrius is leaving it up to me—more or less.
Doing the house over is *my* project, and I have
almost a free hand.'

'Really?' They were upstairs by then, in Grace's
rooms. She wanted to show her surprise, but it
wouldn't have been tactful.

'I know, it's great, isn't it? I'm enjoying it, I'm
interested in interior design. I——' She broke off,
her expression changing. ''Course, I know why he's

letting me do it. It's to keep me quiet. He just wants to keep me out of his hair.'

She looked straight at the elder girl. Her resentment of her brother was evident, but Grace could hardly say what she herself thought about him. It was one thing for Melissa to resent him, quite another to let her own dislike be known. 'Oh, I'm sure you're exaggerating,' she said laughingly.

'I am not! Worse still, now I've lost my licence I'm trapped. Don't you see? I'm going to be a prisoner in that house. It's so far flung I don't see how I'm going to get away without relying on *him* to drive me. Which he won't.'

'There are such things as taxis, you know. Even out here!'

'Do you know what he suggested? That I should get a bike. A bike! Did you ever?'

'What's wrong with that? By the way, do you ride? Horses, I mean.'

'No.' Melissa flopped into a chair. 'Why?'

'Because we keep a couple. I—would you like to learn?'

She brightened, and looked delighted. 'Yes, I'd love to. Demetrius can ride, but he's never offered to teach me.'

Grace had put herself on the spot. She hadn't been thinking of teaching Melissa herself, she'd been thinking of recommending someone at the local stables. Oh, well. Why not? 'All right, I'll give you your first lesson on Sunday—if you're free.'

'What about tomorrow? Do you work Saturdays?'

'The salon's open till lunch time on Saturdays, and we close all day Tuesdays. I don't always go in but—in any case, Sunday would be better for me.'

'No, I didn't mean that. I wondered if you'd like to come over and look at my car tomorrow? In the afternoon?'

'Yes, OK. About what time?'

'Any time after lunch. May I use your bathroom before we go downstairs?'

'Of course. I'll see you in the drawing-room. Can you find your way back?'

'Grace, the house isn't *that* big!'

Demetrius was alone when Grace went down. Their eyes met and clashed. She lowered herself into a chair, asking what had happened to her father.

'He's taking a telephone call in his study.' There was a hint of amusement in his voice. 'Must be something urgent.'

She shrugged. 'It often is.'

'I suppose you share your father's politics?' He was surveying her openly, his eyes moving slowly over her from top to toe, then lingering on her legs.

'This may come as a shock to you, but I'm apolitical these days.'

His dark, heavy eyebrows went up. 'This, from the daughter of a Member of Parliament?'

'What shall we say, that I'm the teetotalling daughter of a drunken father, so to speak? I'm not interested any more. All my life I've heard politics, politics, politics and it all seems like a game to me.'

'A very serious game, Grace.'

She tossed her head back, wishing someone would join them, for the two of them had nothing to say to each other. 'I'm coming over to look at Melissa's car tomorrow afternoon. Did she tell you I'm interested in buying it?'

'I'm glad to hear it. It's a good buy. Of course, it's entirely her business.' His face tightened. 'She's responsible for the vehicle.' He paused, shook his head slightly. 'Do you know why it's for sale?'

Grace smiled. 'She lost her licence for twelve months. Drinking and driving.'

'Speeding.' He almost hissed the word. 'Not only was she half plastered, she was doing one hundred and twenty down the motorway.'

It was no smiling matter, Grace knew that, but she couldn't wipe the smile off her face. His annoyance was delighting her. Very lightly she told him, 'Well, we've all been eighteen at some point or other.'

The words had barely left her mouth when she was jumped on. 'Eighteen? Eighteen? When I was eighteen I didn't have a car of my own. When I was eighteen I was not merely earning my own living but running a business. If you think——'

'Demetrius.' It was Melissa, speaking from the doorway. 'I'm back now, so you'd better stop talking about me.'

'Sit down and shut up! Since you managed to get our name mentioned in the newspapers, since your irresponsibility is no secret to anyone, you can hardly complain if I talk about it.'

Melissa sat, her eyes moving to Grace as if to say, 'You see?'

Grace saw. She saw a man who was intolerant, who had no idea how it felt to be eighteen in today's world, and lacking confidence. Pointedly she asked, 'How long is it since your mother died, Melissa?'

'She died when I was twelve.'

'And what happened then?'

'Demetrius put me in a boarding-school. I was living in Greece at the time, but he brought me back here and put me in a convent school in Derbyshire.'

'Which you enjoyed?'

'Which I hated! I was as lonely as hell.'

Demetrius rolled his eyes at the expression. 'And much good the convent did you.' He glanced at his watch, a surreptitious glance but Grace caught it. Was he bored to death? Whatever, he dismissed the subject of his sister and Grace assumed he had missed the point she had been trying to make. The girl was still lonely, couldn't he see that?

When they left at a little after eleven, Grace went up to bed thinking about them, about both of them. Oddly enough, at some point during the evening she had felt a twinge of sympathy for Demetrius Knight, in spite of his hardness. He might not know how to handle his young sister, but he was by no means indifferent to her. He was intolerant, impatient and overly strict, but he did care, that much was obvious.

On the one hand she found herself wanting to help, if she could, on the other hand she wanted to keep away from them, both of them. It would be wiser not to get involved with her new neighbours. And then she remembered the riding lessons for Melissa.

It was too late. She was already involved.

CHAPTER THREE

'AND finally,' Melissa said with a flourish, 'the *pièce de résistance!*'

'But—this is amazing! I'm impressed, Melissa. Boy, am I impressed!'

'Do you like it?'

'Like it? I love it!' Grace spoke truthfully. She gazed around the half-finished pool room, shaking her head in wonder. Melissa had such style, taste, flair, such—*imagination!*

The Knights' property was not as old as Allinson Manor; it had been built during the twenties, and it was on three storeys including the attics. Grace knew the building well, although she hadn't actually set foot in it for over two years.

The room they were standing in was new, part of an extension which would house a swimming pool, a sauna, changing room and showers. As for the rest of the house, it was almost unrecognisable. The work in progress was advanced and, while there was still plenty of chaos, would be completed within a matter of weeks. Grace had been given a tour by Melissa, who constantly rejected compliments and credit by saying how much Demetrius' architect had helped her. Or by saying how quick and co-operative the builders were, men who were her brother's employees in his construction business.

Nevertheless, the credit was due to her for her vision. It was she who had seen the extension in her mind's eye to begin with, she who had imagined walls knocked through, rooms made bigger, archways in place. And much more. It was she who had chosen the decorations, the carpets, curtains, lighting and much of the furniture which had yet to be delivered.

Grace had been with her for over an hour. She had seen nothing of Demetrius but she knew he was home. He was in his office, the one room in the house she had not been in. On getting here she had glimpsed his silver Mercedes in the double garage at the back of the house, standing next to the BMW she had come to inspect—which she hadn't yet got round to.

'Have a look around first,' Melissa had said. 'But we won't go in the office, because Demetrius is in there working. It was the room that got first priority, had to be finished first, even before our bedrooms. Heaven forbid he shouldn't have an office in his home!'

This room, the pool room, had been last on the agenda and was partly tiled. That was, the tiling in the pool had been finished, in tiny, blue mosaic tiles which had been imported from Italy. The walls were, as yet, half done, the tiling on the floor not yet started.

'The floor tiling will finish here,' Melissa was saying, moving around and pointing enthusiastically. 'The rest will be carpeted in that blue-grey I showed you on the swatch. Against that far wall there'll be an entire bank of plants, tall, exotic-looking things. We're going to build a bar into that corner, and in this floor space here we'll have— what should I call it? Lounging furniture, something comfy but practical for the surroundings— and that's the one thing I haven't found yet. Beyond the big sliding glass doors, which we can keep open in the summer, of course, there'll be a paved patio with a built-in barbecue and regular sun-loungers.' She broke off, smiling. 'So in the summer, hopefully, we can sunbathe, then nip in here for a dip. I considered an outdoor pool, but decided against it.'

'And Demetrius agreed with you?' Grace was smiling, enjoying her enthusiasm.

'Oh, yes. I told you, everything has been given his seal of approval. We agreed it would be much nicer to be able to use the pool all year round. This is England, after all! Our house in Greece has an outside pool, of course, but it's not as splendid as this place—as this place is going to be, I mean.' She smiled. 'So what do you think of it?'

Grace looked at her, having difficulty equating all she had seen with this eighteen-year-old who had rings on almost every finger, a mop of black curls which looked as if they hadn't seen a comb today, who at the moment was wearing a bright yellow sweatshirt and pink velvet trousers tucked into blue leather boots. 'I think it's gorgeous.'

'What? All of it?'

'All of it.'

'But?'

'But nothing.' Grace couldn't help smiling, Melissa had read something in her eyes.

'Come on, out with it. Which part did you hate?'

'It isn't that, honestly.' She laughed and took the plunge. 'It's just that—well, looking at you, thinking about the sort of clothes you go for, the colours and——'

'Ah! You thought I had no taste.' Melissa was straight to the point, quite unruffled. 'Well, naturally,' she went on, shrugging, hands open, palms up, as if talking to someone a bit dim, 'if this were *my* house, it would be different.'

'It would? But it *is* your house!'

'No. It's my home. For now. I won't be here for ever, will I?'

'I—suppose not.' Grace hadn't thought of that.

'It's Demetrius' house. Oh, he gave me *carte blanche*, but I had to consider him, his taste, didn't I? Compared to me he's conservative. I only presented him with ideas I knew he would like, you see. There's no way he would have gone for the sort of things I'd have come up with if I'd let my imagination have full rein. I mean, I wouldn't decorate my own place like *this*!'

'But——' Astonished, Grace didn't know what to make of her. 'You—you don't like it yourself?'

'Of course I like it.' There was a hint of impatience now. 'Within its context, for the person who owns it, who will live here for ever—I assume. It's what Demetrius considers tasteful.'

What Demetrius considers tasteful. Grace considered it tasteful, too. The house, when finished, would be neither modern nor traditional but something in between, smart but extremely comfortable, luxurious but in no way gaudy or overstated, its colourways warm but in no way drab. 'But you don't?'

'What is taste?' Melissa shrugged. 'Is there really such a thing as bad taste, good taste? Isn't it only a matter of opinion, whatever turns you on? There again, thinking of context, let's take your beauty salon. Now, if I were asked to decorate and furnish a beauty salon, I'd come up with something not unlike what you've done there—all pot plants and

pastels and prettiness. But *personally*,' she added
without apology, 'I found the décor execrable.'

Grace burst out laughing. 'Execrable, eh? But—
right for a beauty salon?'

'Precisely!'

Grace slipped an arm around her shoulders. 'I
think I could use a cup of coffee!'

They were both laughing as they walked back into
the main body of the house, but Grace was also
thinking. Melissa was full of surprises and, not only
that, she was talented. When they reached the
kitchen, she asked her what she planned to do with
her future.

This was met by a blank look. 'My future?
I ... haven't really thought about it.'

It was an evasive answer, her eyes had dropped.
And then she said, almost inaudibly, 'I hope to
marry some day, naturally.'

There was a brief silence. Grace guessed she was
thinking about the boy in Greece, the one Demetrius
had forbidden her to see. 'Fair enough—and in the
meantime? Haven't you thought about a career?
Only I was going to ask whether you'd considered
interior decorating.'

Melissa stared at her. 'Interior decorating? Me?
A career of it?'

Grace nodded, at a loss to understand this dramatic reaction. 'It was just a thought.' A thought
which had clearly never entered the girl's mind. In
fact, Grace didn't know whether it was the idea of
a career in itself which had startled her or the idea
of interior decorating as a career. 'Maybe you'd
like to give it some thought?' She added that because Melissa was nodding slowly now, as if she

had been inspired. She looked pleased, there was a light in her eyes.

'Oh. You're still here.'

Grace bristled at the sound of Demetrius' voice behind her, or rather at his choice of words. So he had been aware of her presence in his house, aware and disapproving, by the sound of it. She turned, her big blue eyes unconsciously challenging. 'Have I overstayed my welcome?'

'Not at all,' he said flatly, as if he couldn't care less. 'Were you about to make coffee, Melissa?'

'I *am* about to make coffee, Demetrius. That is why I am filling the kettle.'

'Put your knives away, little sister. I come in peace.' Unexpectedly he turned to look at Grace. 'Were you like that when you were eighteen?'

She kept an impassive face. 'Like what?'

'Sarcastic. Aggressive. On the defensive.'

She was about to answer evasively, knowing she couldn't risk taking sides openly with these two people. If she did, the situation would become impossible. In truth, she had been all of those things at eighteen, and at nineteen, especially at nineteen— not that she had been able to see it at the time. The difficulty was that she could see now both their points of view. She had quickly weighed the information she had about them so far, and was old enough and wise enough to recognise something more difficult than a mere generation gap. They might be brother and sister, but they were worlds apart.

Demetrius was watching her and, unfortunately, misunderstood her hesitation. 'Then it's as I thought.'

'What is?' She looked at him quickly. 'What do you mean?'

'I mean you obviously haven't changed.' He was leaning against the wall, arms folded, unsmiling. 'Hence your attitude towards me last night.'

'My attitude?' She couldn't believe this! 'I would point out that my attitude towards you last night was determined by your attitude towards me in the salon yesterday. I did not care for being spoken to like that.'

'So you decided to get your own back.'

'So I decided to make you aware of my disapproval.'

'Oh! Pardon me, Lady-of-the-Manor.'

Grace felt a flush creeping up her face. That made two in two days. She lifted her chin and looked him straight in the eye. 'It is precisely *that* that bothers me about you. You simply don't know how to treat me, do you? When you thought I was just a girl behind a counter, you were rude. When you realised who I am, you regretted it. When you realised who I am and what I do for a living, you were full of contempt. And just now, by implication, you're telling me you think I'm a snob. But you're the snob, Mr Knight. An inverted one.'

He had listened to every word with a frown which grew deeper and deeper, bringing his heavy black brows together until they were almost touching, the intensely dark eyes lit with that curious light which she could have sworn meant she was amusing him. He and Melissa had that particular thing in common. 'What a crazy, mixed-up girl you are, if that's what you think!'

She had been right, he was laughing at her now, laughing openly, fully, genuinely. It infuriated her even while she was obliged to acknowledge how damned attractive he looked like that, how damned attractive he was.

'That makes two of you,' he went on, jerking a head in Melissa's direction. 'You and my baby sister.'

Melissa was glaring at him. 'Demetrius——'

He ignored her, spoke over her, his eyes still fixed on his neighbour. 'I just hope you're not going to be a bad influence on the little one. God knows, she's had enough of those.'

'Oh, for heaven's sake . . .' Grace got to her feet. 'I'm going!' She would have, too, had Melissa not spoken her name in a voice that was almost a wail. It sobered Grace; Melissa had been caught in the cross-fire, which was really unfair on her. Thoughts of walking out of this house, never to return, were quelled. Why should she walk out? And hurt Melissa? And let Demetrius get the better of her, drive her away? No! She was made of sterner stuff than that. Besides, she liked Melissa enormously, it was just too bad that her brother was impossible, hateful. One thing was for sure, even if she had had no opinion before meeting him, she would have come to the same conclusion.

And yet . . . and yet, seconds later, she was forced to reconsider. Melissa was shrieking at him and he was saying not a word in response. He was merely looking at her, shaking his head and clearly exercising much patience while she ranted.

'Don't you dare talk to Grace like that! How *can* you? But it's typical, isn't it? You do it to all my friends! I have yet to find a friend who meets with your approval, Demetrius. You criticise everyone I like, you always manage somehow to pull them to pieces or frighten them off. There are times when I hate you, *hate you*, and this is one of them! I'm not going to——'

'Melissa.' The word came from Grace. It came so quietly that it was heard at once. As if snapping out of a trance, Melissa turned to look at her while Demetrius, still leaning against the wall, merely sighed.

Grace didn't say anything else, she didn't need to. The younger girl apologised at once, not to her brother but to Grace.

'I'm sorry. I shouldn't have—I'll make the coffee. Demetrius, I'll bring yours to your office in a moment, if you want to get on.'

There was a short, stony silence. Demetrius turned to look at Grace, his eyebrows raised slightly as if she had done something to impress him. Astonishing her, he smiled at her warmly, before leaving the room as quietly as he had entered it. She turned to look after him as he walked away, wondering what that had been about, wondering what he was like when his sister wasn't present. Present to aggravate, albeit unintentionally, most of the time. She turned back to the table, thoughtful, chatting about the décor in the kitchen solely to keep things smooth, to let Melissa know everything was all right again.

An hour or so later, Demetrius emerged once more and Grace immediately looked at her watch. Was he trying to tell her something? 'I—I'd better go. I've been here too long.'

He said nothing, he was filling the kettle, his back to her and his sister, who reminded Grace about the car.

'But you haven't looked at the car yet.'

'No. I—I'm afraid I've had second thoughts about that.' It was the truth. It had occurred to her that it might not be wise to buy Melissa's car. She was a neighbour and a friend now. If she bought her car second-hand and something went wrong with it . . . well, she wasn't quite sure what she thought, but better to keep business and pleasure separate.

'You have?' Melissa was neither perturbed nor disappointed, just mildly surprised. 'It doesn't matter, I've had several phone calls about it already, and I took their numbers just in case. I'll sell it in no time.'

'Good.' She should have left it at that, she wished she had, but she felt she needed to say something more, to explain. 'To tell you the truth, I'm not sure I can afford it, really.'

There was a bark of laughter from the other end of the kitchen and Demetrius turned round, a cynical look on his face. 'Can't afford it? Is that the best you can come up with, Grace? Surely you could buy that car with one week's pocket money from your daddy?'

To her horror, she felt the immediate sting of tears behind her eyes. She quickly glanced down at the table, willing herself not to let them be seen. Demetrius Knight had not angered her this time, he had hurt her. She knew it was stupid to feel like that, when he didn't begin to know her, how her mind worked, how there was a broad streak of independence in her or—or anything at all. Yet she was hurt and very upset. But she was *damned* if she'd let him know it!

Very quietly, knowing that she really had to leave now, and the sooner the better, she simply appeared to agree with him because it was the easiest thing to do, the quickest way to shut him up. 'You're probably right. Anyway, I really must be off now. I'll—ring you later to make arrangements for tomorrow, Melissa.'

She left, without further ado, without any fuss. She got in to her car and headed down the drive leading to the lane that linked the two houses. There was no short-cut home, their grounds had boundaries on all sides.

Only when she got to the lane did she stop, to think. She switched off the engine and clamped both hands on the steering wheel. She was breathing deeply again; she had to steady herself, she had to think. The best thing to do, clearly, was to avoid the company of Demetrius Knight whenever possible. Their mutual dislike had nothing to do with his sister, that was also clear. Grace knew, now, what he really thought about her; his last remark had made it very plain: 'You could buy that car with one week's pocket money from your daddy.'

Obviously he thought her a brat, rich and spoiled. Rich and spoiled and, no doubt, simply amusing herself with her business. A business in which she 'exploited' the idle, the overweight and the ugly. Those had been his words, had they not? No doubt he assumed her clientele were rich people like herself, rich and spoiled. Oh, how little he knew!

'Damn the man!' The suppressed tears got suddenly out of control, and came streaming down her face. And with them came anger, *anger*, the likes of which she had not known for five years. How *dare* he make assumptions about her, *any* assumptions? So he had 'come from nothing', as her father had put it, while she had been born with a silver spoon in her mouth. So what? Did that automatically invoke his prejudice? His *contempt*? Maybe he presumed she'd had no problems in her life, that being born rich meant an easy passage, self-indulgence and fulfilment of—of whims!

She fired the engine and slammed the gear lever into first. It was no use sitting there, she wasn't going to calm down in a matter of minutes. She might as well go home and work off her anger, clean her bedroom or something.

It was going to take hours, if not days, to get over her latest encounter with Demetrius Knight.

CHAPTER FOUR

'YOU'RE not enjoying yourself, are you, Melissa?' Grace watched her dismount; there was no way she was going to make a good rider. Anyone could be taught how to ride, but not everyone took to it easily, not everyone had a feeling for horses, and if one were afraid of them... 'Why are you grinning like that? Did you think I didn't know?'

This was their fourth attempt, the fourth Sunday afternoon they had spent together—in the grounds of Allinson Manor. 'Melissa?'

'I'm not a quitter, you know. It's just that—well, I don't really like it.'

'I know. So there's no point. We'll have to think again. You're going to need something to do in your spare time once that house of yours is in order.'

'I've sent off for some prospectuses.' Melissa was a few paces behind Grace as they led the horses back to the stables, looking at her and obviously expecting a response.

'Prospectuses? You mean for university?'

'University, polytechnics, anywhere. I've written to several places.' She shook her head in frustration. 'You've forgotten! I'm making enquiries about courses on interior design and decoration.'

'Oh! Oh, Melissa, that's marvellous! That *is* exciting. Come on, let's see to the horses and then we can have some coffee and talk about it.' Grace was genuinely pleased. 'What does Demetrius think of the idea?'

The younger girl's expression changed, the smile dropped from her face. 'I haven't told him yet.'

'But—why ever not?'

'I—I don't know how he'd react. He's a strange man, you know, he doesn't trust me. And he has a wicked temper at times.' She sighed. 'I'm not being dramatic, it's true. He's far more English than I am in many ways, but—he is half-Greek and when he gets passionate about something, he gets passionate. You've never seen him in a temper. It's not a pretty sight.'

Grace did not pursue the conversation. She hadn't been in the Knights' house again, she had stuck firmly to her resolve about avoiding Demetrius. There had been a few occasions during the last three weeks when Melissa had phoned her in the early evening, asking her over. 'Demetrius is in his office and probably won't come out before bedtime. How about coming round for a couple of hours?'

Grace had declined, but had offered to collect her and bring her to her home for the evening instead, for she knew Melissa was lonely. She had picked her up and had delivered her home again— without setting foot in her brother's house. As far as she was concerned, it was an arrangement that worked very well, but Demetrius Knight obviously had other ideas...

On the following Wednesday, some time after Grace had driven his sister home, he came round to see her. She was just going upstairs to bed when the doorbell rang. She hurried to answer it, at a loss to imagine who it could be.

'Mr Knight! I—well, I certainly didn't expect——'

'Demetrius. I know, you certainly didn't expect to find me standing on your doorstep.'

The way he had finished the sentence for her made her bristle, but she said nothing.

'May I come in?'

'Of course.' She stepped aside, her inbred good manners alone preventing her from adding, 'If you must.' She led the way to the drawing-room and flicked on the lights. 'I hope this won't take too long, I was just on my way to bed——'

'I realise that,' he said, 'and I'm sorry to disturb you.'

He wasn't at all sorry, he settled in the armchair by the fireplace, looking perfectly at home and as though he was there for the duration. 'I want to talk to you about Melissa.'

'I realise that,' she said, mimicking his own words, his carelessness. 'There's nothing else you could wish to talk to me about.'

Suddenly he smiled, managing somehow, once again, to make her regret her clever retort. 'I wouldn't be too sure about that. You've hardly given me a chance, have you?'

'Mr Knight——'

'Demetrius. Why so aggressive, Grace? Has my sister influenced you so much that you're incapable of gauging my character for yourself? This is precisely why I'm here,' he added, his eyes fixed firmly on hers as she sat down some distance from him. 'I want to say that I'm grateful to you for entertaining Melissa—but I find your avoidance of me both childish and aggravating.'

Grace denied the accusation, even though it was the truth. She flushed, hating herself for it and wondering how it was he always managed to do this to her. 'Avoidance? I haven't——'

'You haven't set foot in my house for almost a month. You've collected Melissa and you've delivered her—as you did this evening—and tonight when you refused her invitation to come in for a nightcap, I decided I'd come over and sort you out.'

'Sort me——' She couldn't believe what she was hearing. Sort her out? As for Melissa—well, she had obviously been questioned when she got indoors!

'That's what I said. Now then, perhaps you'll tell me what I've done to offend you?'

She was about to do just that but, before she had a chance he held up a hand, silencing her, taking the wind out of her sails. 'Think before you answer. Try to leave my sister's opinion of me out of it.'

Newly offended, she shot to her feet. 'This is pointless. It's quite obvious you're incapable of holding a civilised conversation. You're the aggressive one, you're also extremely rude. You seem to take pleasure in insulting my intelligence!'

For a long moment nothing was said. He stared at her, as if he'd thought her incapable of such an outburst. When at last he broke the silence, he smiled appreciatively. 'Well, well, it seems there's more to you than meets the eye. Speaking of which, may I say how beautiful you look when you're riled?'

'You may say whatever you like—but not to me. I've heard enough. Please leave, Mr Knight.'

'Demetrius.'

'For heaven's sake——'

'Are you coming to the party?'

Grace glared at him, at a loss to understand for a moment. He looked so at home in that armchair, so unruffled, so *amused* by all this. 'What party?' she snapped.

'Our housewarming.'

'Oh.' She sat down again, feeling idiotic. Melissa had gone on about this, about how she had persuaded Demetrius to throw the party. 'But naturally he had to be snide,' she had added, 'and spoilt it by telling me not to invite my crazy friends from London. Honestly! Just because they smoke grass...'

Of course Grace was invited, but she had not yet made up her mind whether to go. It was a few weeks away yet, over Easter, by which time the Knights' house would be finished.

'Miss Gracie?' The housekeeper interrupted them before anything else could be said. She was standing in the doorway, looking apologetic. 'I'm so sorry, I wasn't sure whether I heard voices. I saw the lights and... well, I came down to get some hot milk and I wondered whether you'd like some? Good evening, Mr Knight.'

'Good evening to you, Matilda. How are you?'

'I'm fine, thank you, sir. And you? How's your house coming along?'

'Very nicely. You must come and see it when it's finished. In fact, we're having a housewarming party and Miss Grace will be there, and Sir Nigel, of course. And you'll be more than welcome, Matilda.'

Grace watched the exchange with an amusement she hid. Matty, bless her, was being charmed by the man! Could she see no further than his handsome face? Couldn't she see what he was really like? Apparently not.

'No drink for me, Matty,' Grace interrupted at the earliest opportunity. 'And Mr Knight was just leaving.'

'Not at all,' he said smoothly. 'I'm in no hurry.' He turned to the housekeeper. 'I'd love some coffee, if it's no trouble.'

He was assured by the retreating Matty that it was no trouble at all. Grace folded her arms across her chest and waited. Silence reigned.

'Well?'

'Well what?'

'The party, Grace. How about it?'

She let out a slow breath. 'Didn't you just tell my housekeeper I would be there? It seems you've taken me for granted.'

'And do you mind that?'

'I mind very much. If you knew me better, you would know that taking me for granted is a mistake.'

He inclined his head, his interest aroused—which was the last thing she had intended to do. 'How about giving me the chance?'

'What?'

'To get to know you better. Come out to dinner with me tomorrow.'

'No, thank you.'

Demetrius laughed. 'That isn't very neighbourly, is it?'

She was unmoved. The fact that she was going out to dinner with Rodney Featherstone the following evening was irrelevant, she was simply not interested in going out with this man. 'Perhaps it isn't. I will, however, come to your housewarming party—because Melissa wants me to. And that reminds me, Thomas will be home over Easter, I take it he's invited, too?'

'Thomas? Ah, yes, your brother. Of course he's invited.'

'There's nothing to say he'll come, mind you; my brother isn't exactly the partying type.'

'What type is he?'

She sighed, feeling that she had no choice but to sit here; Matty had just walked in with his coffee and that meant at least another fifteen minutes. Still, her irritation had subsided now the conversation had taken a more pleasant, and neutral, turn. 'I suppose he's something of a boffin.'

'You mean a mad scientist?'

'You're getting the picture. Very much an academic.'

'How old is he?'

'Twenty-seven.'

'And you, Grace? How old are you?'

'Twenty-four.' Her impatience was resurfacing, it wasn't his questions so much as the way he was looking at her. His admiration of her physical appearance was unconcealed and it was also unwanted. 'How come you don't know anything about me and Thomas?'

'Why should I?'

'My father——'

'Nigel has never discussed his children with me, except to say that he's proud of them.'

'I'm glad to hear that.'

'That he hasn't discussed you?'

'That he's proud of us.' Her eyes closed. It hadn't always been the case, heaven knew that. Not as far as she was concerned, anyway! 'Well, I'm proud of my brother, too.'

There was another silence. It felt awkward to Grace, but Demetrius evidently didn't feel that way. He was looking at her now as if he had never seen her before, as if he were reassessing her. Quite suddenly he said, 'By rights, I should have had two brothers.'

'I—what do you mean?'

'My mother had two more sons after me. They both died within five weeks of birth. She said she thought she'd never get over that, having two of them die. She said she gave up, she'd always wanted a daughter but she wasn't going to risk having another baby. Melissa came along unexpectedly, very unexpectedly, years later when it was almost too late. My mother was forty-three when Melissa was born. I was eighteen by then, and working for Dad.'

That he should volunteer information of this nature surprised Grace. She knew about her neighbours' background, she thought the story both romantic and sad, but she hadn't known about the two babies. 'Your parents met in Greece during World War Two, didn't they?'

'That's right. My mother's immediate family, all of them, had been killed. She got a passage to England at the end of the war and married my father in his home town, in Devon. Dad went into business with an ex-army friend, as a builders' merchant. But his friend died and so Dad kept the business going alone. It was just in a small way, he didn't make much money, he wasn't ambitious except to see that his family were sheltered and fed.

'When Melissa was six months old my father was killed on a building site. He was making a delivery and there was an accident. He was crushed to death. The shock almost killed my mother. When Melissa was two she took her to live in Greece—home, as she still thought of it. She went back to Athens, where she'd been born. I can't say I approved of that, but I could hardly prevent her, any more than she could insist I went with her. I'd been running Dad's business for over two years and had expanded it.'

In spite of herself, Grace had to smile. Expanded it, he'd said. He had made more money than his father ever had. 'How old were you then?'

'Twenty.'

'And you've come a long way since.' She was still smiling, unaware how interested she had become until she heard herself saying, 'Tell me more.'

He shrugged, 'That's about it, really.'

'That's not the end of the story. Your mother took the two-year-old Melissa to Athens, and I take it you supported them from afar. Did she still have friends there?'

'Some, and a few distant relatives—well, cousins, second cousins and the like, a few aunts and uncles who were much older, all of whom are poor. I visited occasionally and, when I could afford to, I bought her a house. Then, in time, a better house.'

'The one with the outdoor swimming pool,' Grace added, smiling at his look of surprise. 'No, I didn't know the full story, just part of it. So, when your mother died you took Melissa away from Greece?'

'I had no choice, she could hardly have lived in the house alone. There was no way I would hand her over to relatives, either, not that she'd have liked that.'

'So you sent her to boarding-school, the convent school in Derbyshire.'

He frowned. 'You make that sound like an accusation.'

'Not at all,' she said hastily, sincerely. 'What else could you have done?'

'Quite. I was living in my apartment in London, but I travelled around a lot in those days. It would have been impractical to keep her with me. Besides, what did I know about twelve-year-old girls?'

'I wonder,' Grace said gently, not wishing to antagonise him when they were finally managing to communicate, 'how much you know about eighteen-year-old girls.'

In the face of his silence she thought she had failed to keep the peace. He put his coffee-cup down, got to his feet and crossed over to where she was sitting, looking down at her. She got up and took two paces to the side. 'Look, I only meant——'

'It's all right,' he said softly, his hand reaching to encircle her wrist. 'No offence taken. You're right. I wonder, too. I find that I understand females very well indeed...when they're a little older than eighteen.'

She looked down at her arm, where his hand lay in a grip that was unnecessarily tight. Suddenly he pulled her closer to him, so close that she could see for the first time quite how intensely beautiful his eyes were. 'Demetrius——'

'So how about our dinner date?'

'No—thank you. It's very sweet of you but——'

'Don't patronise me, just say yes.'

She had to look away then, there was too much information coming at her all at once. His nearness was bothering her, his hand felt as if it were burning into her flesh, and on top of all this there was the effect his conversation had had on her. He had surprised her by opening up like that, he wasn't the unreasonable brute she had thought him, far from it. But even so... 'No.' It came out firmly, in fact she didn't know why she had hesitated. She might have had to reassess this man, but in honesty she still couldn't say she liked him, certainly not enough to go out with him alone.

So why was it that his lack of insistence bothered her? Why did she feel let down when he merely shrugged and said he would see himself out? Worst of all, at the last minute she heard herself saying something about taking a raincheck. 'Perhaps—perhaps some other time, Demetrius.'

He was at the door of the drawing-room by then. He didn't even turn to look back at her. 'Perhaps. Goodnight, Grace.'

Over the following few days she went over that encounter with him several times. She heard nothing from him or his sister. She was alone in the house at the weekend; Matilda had Sundays off and had gone to visit her sister, Sir Nigel was spending the weekend in London, which was unusual, very. It was something else worth a thought. Was her father seeing his lady-friend? If so, why didn't he simply say so? He had given no explanation for his staying in town. Not for the first time in her life, Grace thought people funny, strange. So often they made

problems for themselves by making things unnecessarily complex. What was it someone had once
said? 'I'm an old man and I've had many worries
in my life, most of which never happened.'

Her business was closed all day Tuesdays, and
she went into London to do some shopping. Spring
was just around the corner, and the shops were full
of new fashions, new colours. She bought several
dresses, a new suit and two pairs of shoes.

As if obliging only her, the weather on
Wednesday was fine. The wind had finally abated
and the sky was blue. It was March and actually
felt as though spring had sprung. She put on one
of her new dresses, a deep blue shirtwaister in fine
cotton, popped a jacket in her car just for in-
surance, and drove to Wokingham in a very good
mood.

She got to the salon at eight-twenty-five, turned
on the lights and switched switches on the telephone answering-machine, always the first job of
the day. The first message was the cancellation of
Mrs Evans' appointment for an eyelash tint, which
was not exactly serious, and the next message was
from Demetrius Knight.

Grace looked at the machine as if it had just
bitten her, played the message through for a second
and then a third time. The voice was crystal clear
and businesslike: 'Hello, Grace. This is Demetrius
Knight, I'm calling at eight a.m., Wednesday. I'm
not sure what time you open, but perhaps you'd
call me back.' There followed his telephone number,
an extension number and then, 'I'd like to talk to
you. I was wondering if you'd have lunch with me
today.'

'Lunch?' She spoke aloud, as if expecting the little grille on the machine to offer an explanation. What explanation could there be? And then she realised. She sat down, groaning, cursing Melissa.

She, Grace, had exercised as much diplomacy as she could. She had tried to be friendly and supportive to Melissa, but she had *not* interfered in her relationship with her brother or in any other way. Had she? Or had she? It was she who had put the idea of interior decorating into her head.

So there was going to be trouble. Demetrius wanted to talk to her, and she didn't need three guesses what it was about. Promptly, she picked up the telephone and dialled. There was no point in putting this off, she didn't even want to. Melissa had taken her advice, clearly, and had told Demetrius what she was up to.

A crisp voice answered. 'DKK Holdings, may I help you?'

'Extension nineteen, please.'

She was put straight through, and was surprised when the extension was answered, not by a secretary, but by Demetrius himself. 'Oh! I—was expecting a first line of defence.'

'Who is this?' The voice was clipped.

'Grace Allinson. I—got your message.'

'Grace!' The tone changed at once, astonishing her in its friendliness. 'This is a private extension, it comes directly to me.' There was a pause, then, without preamble, 'Can you manage lunch? I wondered if you'd mind coming here?'

She hardly knew what to say. She was actually pleased by the prospect of seeing him, it surprised her how much so, but she didn't want him to know it. 'I suppose I could, but—I mean, is it really necessary?'

Silence. Just one word, as if his feelings were hurt: 'Necessary?'

'I mean, what I meant was——'

'Is your dislike of me still so strong, Grace?'

'Well, I mean . . .' Why was she feeling guilty? It was ridiculous. 'I mean, why not?'

'That's better. This building is very easy to find, there's an excellent local company who cater for us from time to time, boardroom lunches and all that. Why don't you pop over and have a leisurely lunch with me?'

Was he mocking her? She honestly couldn't tell. What was he up to? 'Give me your address and tell me what time I should come.'

He did, and hung up.

She was still looking at the phone when Jillian walked in. 'Morning, Grace. Isn't it nice? I think spring has finally . . . are you all right?'

Grace looked up, totally bemused—partly at herself. Unthinking, she said, 'I have a luncheon appointment.'

'Oh.' Jillian beamed broadly. 'I thought someone had died.'

That was typical of her, and it was enough to snap Grace out of her reverie. She laughed as Jillian headed for the tiny kitchen and the coffee percolator.

At noon precisely she set off for Bracknell and rehearsed en route what she would say to Demetrius. It wasn't difficult, didn't need much thinking about. If he wanted to know why Melissa had taken her time in telling him about college, she would be straight with him. 'Because she's scared of you sometimes,' she would say. To hell with it, it was the truth. If he didn't like it, tough! In any case, he probably knew it already.

The building in which his head offices were was familiar to Grace and simple to find. It was big and impressive, with a tinted glass façade. She parked in the private car park, walked briskly through the automatic doors in the main entrance, and discovered that DKK Holdings were on the second floor, the whole of the second floor.

In reception, she was escorted immediately to the boss's office, where he was there to receive her, his door open. He stood, towering over her, dressed in an immaculate navy blue suit, a whiter-than-white shirt and a dark red tie. Very sombre and... conservative, to use Melissa's word. He bowed slightly and gestured for her to precede him. 'It's good of you to come, Grace. Do sit down.'

She was about to sit in the outsized, black leather swivel chair facing his desk, thought better of it and sat on a matching settee against one wall.

'Quite right, too,' he was smiling. 'You haven't come here to be interviewed.'

Hadn't she? Then why was she here? She tensed a little when he sat next to her, about two feet from her, on the settee. She wished she had opted for the swivel chair. He was looking at her intently, there was no smile on his face now. It had vanished as quickly as it had appeared, and his eyes were flitting over her. 'You're looking lovely. New dress?'

Grace blinked, shook herself. 'Demetrius——'

'Oh, come on, now. Don't get uppity with me again. Did my remark offend? I make no apology if it did,' he added, 'I'm just interested to know how your mind works.' In the face of her silence he grinned, an enchanting and positively roguish grin. 'Well, now...' He settled himself into the corner of the settee, hooked one long leg over the other and raised his black brows expectantly. 'Let's try again. You're looking lovely today, Grace. But then you always do. New dress?'

There was only one thing she could do. She laughed. 'Yes, and thank you.'

'A drink?'

'I'd love one. A gin and tonic.'

He was on his feet, opening a cabinet which appeared to be solid mahogany. 'Ice?'

'No ice.'

Grace looked around as he poured the drinks; she took in the dark green of the carpet, the pale colour of the walls, the paintings hung around, the massive mahogany desk and the furniture. There were no filing cabinets in here, just the desk and the three telephones on it to make it an office rather than a masculine sort of sitting-room. But, even as she occupied herself thus, she was deciding she would simply play things by ear. She took the glass he offered, raised it, said 'Good health,' and left the ball in his court.

'You think I want to talk to you about Melissa, don't you?'

'Naturally.'

'Well, you're wrong. I want to talk to you about you. I owe you an apology.'

Her eyes opened wider. If she had known how lovely they looked, how blue in the light from the windows, she would have understood why suddenly he seemed to have lost his drift. 'As I was saying, I—owe you an apology, and it's long overdue.'

She looked away. If she had thrown her drink down, it might have explained why suddenly she felt . . . felt a little light-headed. But she hadn't even sipped her drink. It was seconds before she realised what it was. It was him. His nearness was making her uncomfortable—again. She looked back at him. If she reached out a hand, she could touch him. He had sat closer to her after getting their drinks, and she was catching the faintest whiff of aftershave, something tangy and fresh and masculine. But, worse than that, she was seeing in this light that his eyes were very nearly black. The light was catching them and they seemed fathomless, gorgeous, and they were fixed on hers so intently she feared he would be able to read her mind. With an effort she broke their contact, looking away again, only to find her gaze moving over the length of his legs, over the hard muscles of his thighs beneath the dark material of his suit.

He smiled, that full, warm smile which changed his face, softened it somehow, and gave her the benefit of beautiful, white teeth. Then he reached over and covered her hand with his. It was the briefest touch, yet the contact made her jump; it was as if she had been touched by an electric current . . . one which attracted rather than repelled. She was certain he had felt it, too, because he withdrew his hand quickly and she saw a flash of something in his eyes. Surprise? Bemusement?

Dismayed, she was obliged to acknowledge how much she was physically attracted to him. She hadn't lived to be twenty-four without being able to recognise physical attraction—not when it was staring her in the face. In fact it had been there from the start, she was forced to admit that, too.

Something had leapt inside her the very first time she had set eyes on him, but she had been too annoyed to acknowledge it. She reminded herself of that now, of that annoyance and of all the others, and tried to get this meeting back on to a business-like footing.

She looked at her watch, 'Suppose you get to the point, Demetrius?'

He was not put out; his eyes narrowed slightly, giving her the impression that he knew very well that she was trying hard to remain aloof—and that she was failing. 'I had dinner with your father in London on Monday. He talked about you. I have to say I encouraged him to.'

'So?'

'So I owe you an apology, as I've said.'

About to ask what he meant, she was pre-empted by the sound of a buzzer on his desk. Demetrius got up to answer it. 'It seems we're all set for lunch.' He gestured towards the door.

Grace picked up her glass and followed him down a thickly carpeted corridor, through a door marked 'Boardroom' and into a room leading off it, a private dining-room. A table was set for two, with a crisp white linen cloth, Waterford crystal and gleaming cutlery, in the midst of which there were fine china plates covered with paper-thin slices of smoked salmon. In the centre of the table was a small vase containing freesias, which were expensive at this time of year and, as it happened, her favourite flowers. Beside that there was a little solid silver bell, and in a stand by the side of the table an ice-bucket containing a bottle of French champagne—and again, oddly enough, it was her favourite. Demetrius Knight liked the good things in life.

'This—this looks lovely, Demetrius. Why the champagne?'

'In the hope that you'll accept my apology and we can start afresh.'

Grace smiled. 'I'm sure I will, if you'll tell me what the apology's for!'

'I misjudged you. It was wrong of me when I made that remark about buying a car with pocket money from your father. It hurt you, I heard it in your voice and I understand why now. You see, my first impressions were that you were spoiled and an intellectual lightweight. All I can say in self-defence is that I resented your animosity towards me the night I had dinner at the manor. I assumed that Melissa had done a fine old job of running me down, and I was annoyed that you didn't wait to judge for yourself—as I said to you last week. Well, I apologise, Grace.'

She was stuck for words. He had delivered his apology and his explanation without taking his eyes from hers. She liked that, she liked his openness, his honesty—and most of all she liked the fact that he was big enough to say he'd been wrong.

She looked at the bottle in the ice-bucket, smiling. 'Open the champagne.'

He did, after holding out his hand to her. She took it, shook it, and set about eating her smoked salmon. When they'd finished, Demetrius rang the silver bell and the next course was brought in by an immaculately clad woman in her early fifties, whom Demetrius introduced as his secretary.

When the woman retreated, Grace looked down at her plate and laughed delightedly. 'All right, you'd better tell me more about your conversation with my father. You fished very deeply for your information, didn't you? You've organised my favourite flowers and champagne, my favourite starter, main course—and there'll be no pudding for me. Am I right?'

He was laughing now, outrageous laughter which made her laugh harder. 'Nigel said you never eat afters, you were born without a sweet tooth.'

'Did he now? Go on.'

'He also told me you're a very determined person.'

'That's true.'

'And unpredictable.'

'That's also true.' She was still laughing, but Demetrius sobered. 'Seriously, he told me about your attitude towards your business, all the training you went through. I know the difference between a beautician and a beauty therapist now. I know you financed it wholly by your own efforts, wouldn't take a penny or any kind of help from your father. He admires you for it. And so do I.' There was a pause, one which seemed ominous to Grace. Again she prompted him to go on.

Demetrius looked at her apologetically. 'I'm afraid Nigel went on more than I'd anticipated. He—seemed to enjoy talking about you once he got started and, as I've said, I had encouraged it. Anyway, he told me about Raymond Ferris. I think it still bothers him—I mean, because your relationship with him has never been the same since. I'm quoting, Grace, those were his words.'

Grace was quiet for a long time. She continued to eat, saying nothing, just thinking. She was surprised by her absence of emotion; she was neither embarrassed nor annoyed. In short, she felt nothing at all—nothing except regret at her father's words. It was true, their relationship had not been as close since the episode with Raymond Ferris. She had taken it for granted that it could not be. But was that true? Had she made an effort to get her relationship with her father back on its old footing? To be good friends with him, as she had once been? Had *he* made an effort? Yes, in fact he had ... She was perturbed, she thought she had forgiven him completely but ... perhaps she hadn't, really. She pushed her empty plate to one side, drank what champagne there was in her glass and accepted Demetrius' offer of a refill.

At the age of nineteen she had vowed never to speak to her father again. She had been so young for her years, more so than Melissa was. After leaving school at eighteen she, too, had drifted for a while. After finally making up her mind what she wanted to do, she enrolled on the course in beauty therapy in South London, left home and took a flat with a co-student. Within a month she had met and fallen head over heels, *blindly* in love, with Raymond Ferris, whose radical political ideas had fascinated her at the time. He was thirty-one, out of work, and purported to be a Communist. He had been unlike anyone Grace had met before, very unlike! Years younger than he, she thought him as wise as God. She told him everything there was to know about herself and her family and, when he asked her to marry him, she didn't think twice. She had known him two weeks and two days. She said yes.

And then the trouble began. She took him home the weekend he proposed, and her family were horrified by what they saw as a bearded lout who simply didn't want to find work. It made no difference to her, she was Raymond's for ever and ever. Their relationship lasted a grand total of five weeks, and during that time they had only one fight.

It was soon after they'd met, the night he made a very serious attempt to get her in to bed. Grace was already in love with the man, but she was afraid of consummating that love. Her very proper up-bringing told her it was wrong outside marriage, and at nineteen she believed that, but there were other considerations, too. Like the possibility of getting pregnant, fear and lack of experience and the possibility that, if Raymond had his wicked way with her, he would then drop her immediately.

So she fought him off, told him she thought it was wrong. He laughed and called her adorable. Shortly after that he proposed and, when she accepted, insisted they marry quickly because 'he couldn't hold out for too long'. Couldn't wait to get his hands on her. What he had really meant was that he couldn't wait to get his hands on her money.

Unbeknown to Grace, her father went to see Raymond and offered him a sum of money in cash to leave her alone. She learned later that Raymond had bartered for more, for double, in fact. Sir Nigel paid up...and Raymond vanished. He left London altogether...and he left a note for Grace, a note which was handed to her by the porter in college. She could remember to this day the exact wording of it, the cruelty of it. 'Dear Baby Grace, Your father seems to think it won't do his political career any good at all if I become his son-in-law. He's given me a fat sum of money which will keep me in grass for a long time. How could I resist? I will miss you, though, you're a real sweetie-pie.'

'Charming!'

Horrified, Grace almost dropped the glass she was holding. She hadn't merely remembered the wording of that note, she had spoken it aloud!

CHAPTER FIVE

Grace shrugged. A moment's consideration had told her it didn't matter that she'd spoken aloud. Demetrius knew the story—or as much as her father had known of it. 'We live and learn.' She raised an eyebrow, her head cocking to one side as she looked straight at him. 'So you see, I'm not a snob. I was on the verge of marrying the scum of the earth—or so I thought.'

'I'm sorry I was privy to all that,' he said quietly, 'your father just came out with it, and I could hardly stop him in mid-sentence.'

'I'm glad he told you,' she said honestly, 'because this has given me something to think about. I resented his intervention at the time. I was that young, that stupid, I thought he'd ruined my future, taken my love away.' She looked heavenward, provoking a smile. 'The awful thing is, I don't think I've completely forgiven him.'

'But he did you a favour, surely you can see that?'

'Of course I can see it! What I'm trying to tell you,' she went on, leaning towards him, her deep blue eyes growing darker, 'is that I'm still harbouring some resentment, after all this time. It's pathetic of me, but I realise now that I've always resented the very fact of his interfering in my life. Never mind whether he did me a favour or not,' she added passionately. 'Do you see? I've never actually *told* him I've forgiven him, forgiven him for doing what he simply had to do, what was right for

77

me. I'm going to talk to him, Demetrius, and I'm very grateful to you that we've had this conversation.'

His smile was slow; it reached his eyes, bringing that light into them, causing little crinkles in the corners. 'You're quite a girl, Grace. The more I learn, the more I like.'

She was transfixed in the ensuing silence, ridiculously pleased by what he had said, by what she could see in his eyes. 'And you, you're...' She looked away, embarrassed suddenly. He was what? She didn't know, couldn't finish the sentence because she didn't know what she'd been about to say. 'I—I'd better be going.'

'Oh, no, you don't! You might not have a sweet tooth, but I know you like coffee. Now come on, you're not going to run away from me when we've just made friends.'

Grace couldn't help laughing. But she shouldn't have laughed; she regretted it because, without any warning, with the quickest, smoothest of movements, Demetrius caught hold of her chin and brushed his lips over hers.

They both froze, their faces merely an inch apart, his hand still on her, warm and firm against her skin. Then he moved again, and his mouth was on hers in earnest and there wasn't a thing she could do to prevent it—because it never occurred to her to try. She was blushing when he released her, all too soon, blushing in confusion and—and in her acute physical awareness of him.

Just like the silly teenager she had once been, she said something trite, unable simply to accept what had happened... what was happening. 'Do you do that to all your new friends?'

Demetrius didn't smile, didn't seem to think her remark trite at all, and he answered her seriously. 'Only the ones I'm attracted to.' His eyes locked on to hers for several seconds before he picked up the silver bell and shattered the sudden silence.

Before they had finished their coffee, however, she knew she had to get a move on.

'Must you?' He saw her glancing at her watch, though she was by no means obvious about it.

'I'm sorry, really I am, but I must go. I've got appointments——'

'Yes. Of course.'

There was a pause, and Grace waited, hoping he would again invite her to dine with him—out, alone. But he didn't. When they got up and he saw her out, he merely said, 'By the way, did Melissa tell you she's thinking of going to college in the autumn—to take a course in interior design and decoration?'

She wasn't sure how to answer. 'Er—well, that sounds good to me. What do you think about it?'

'I think it's great. She is talented, you know, what she's done with that house is—but of course you know, it was you who suggested a career in that field.' To her relief, he added, 'And I'm very grateful to you, Grace. She needs a goal in life and she's much brighter than one might think, she left school with good qualifications...'

Grace drove back to The Beauty Parlour in a state of...in a state. Full stop. She shouldn't have been driving at all, she was feeling heady from the champagne and from—from her experience with Demetrius, heady with pleasure and relief at his reaction to Melissa's news, heady with...with all she had learned about him. He had apologised for mis-

judging her. Well, she had certainly misjudged him,
too; he was in fact a man of integrity, of tact, he
had a capacity for understanding which she would
never have given him credit for. The way he had
listened to her ramblings about Raymond Ferris and
her feelings towards her father...

But, beyond the relief and the pleasure, the af-
terglow of the encounter, there was disappointment
because he hadn't asked to see her alone again.

That was soon remedied. No sooner had she got
back to The Beauty Parlour than the telephone
rang—it was Demetrius.

'Two things,' he said, sounding businesslike
again. 'I wanted to check that you got back all right,
and I want to tell you I feel grossly unsatisfied.'

'Unsatisfied?' She had no idea what he was
talking about. 'What do you——'

'I think we have unfinished business.'

Unfinished business? The phrase made her smile.
If he meant that they could happily, easily, have
talked more, he was right.

'Your hesitation,' he said, his voice firm but soft
down the telephone line, 'confirms it. So let's have
dinner tonight. I'll pick you up at—shall we say,
eight o'clock?'

She was smiling, there was no hesitation now.
'Eight o'clock it is.' She put the phone down and
caught herself staring at it again. This time there
was no one to see the look on her face, no one to
tease her about it...but at a little after four o'clock
she came in for plenty of teasing. She was in the
back of the salon when Jillian came for her.

'Grace? Could you come out for a moment? I
think you'll want to know about this straight
away...'

Mystified, Grace followed her to the reception area. On the counter top there was a magnificent arrangement of flowers, displayed in a basket dressed up with ribbons. The accompanying card was in a tiny envelope and Grace read it silently.

'I can't wait until eight,' it said. 'I want to know more and more.'

So did Jillian, she was watching her boss expectantly, but Grace wasn't volunteering anything. She slipped the card into the pocket of her overall and grinned. 'Don't look at me like that, Jillian. This is just a gesture of appreciation from a friend.'

'A friend?'

'A friend.'

Grace laughed and went back to her client. Demetrius Knight was full of surprises. She spent the rest of the day looking forward to eight o'clock, by which time she was ready and waiting in the drawing-room at home. She had taken care with her appearance, having swept her hair into a chignon and chosen to wear a soft, jersey-knit dress in beige.

Demetrius arrived on the dot. He looked her over and smiled approvingly. The flowers he had sent were on the hall table now and she thanked him for them. 'They're beautiful, Demetrius.'

'My pleasure,' he said, his eyes sweeping over her once again. 'Beautiful flowers for a beautiful lady.'

She had no idea where they were going to dine, but she soon guessed; they headed west and in time they drew up at a favourite restaurant of hers, some twenty miles from home. They were shown to a corner table which had a 'reserved' sign on it when they arrived. It was a cosy place with excellent food, a small dance-floor and a trio which played most evenings, tonight being one of them.

Right from the start the evening was a success; although she had changed her opinion about Demetrius, she was still surprised at how very easy he was to talk to. He was witty and amusing, he seemed to know something about everything except, perhaps, the beauty business.

'Aromatherapy?' he said at one point, when she was telling him, at his insistence, about everything they did at the salon. 'What on earth is that?'

'It's a full body massage using essential oils. It's proved to be more popular than I'd expected, actually. It's very good for——'

'I can imagine,' he cut in, grinning. 'I'd like to experience it some time.'

Grace acted as if she was missing the point. 'Really? Well, you may or may not be surprised to learn that we do have one or two male clients. I could book you in with Jillian, if you like, she's very well qualified——'

She got no further. Demetrius threw back his head and laughed. 'That isn't quite what I had in mind—as I'm sure you realise.' His dark eyes were glittering in the candlelight, moving slowly over her. 'I was thinking of a private session with the boss, in my pool room, perhaps, after we've taken a sauna together...'

'Were you, indeed?' She raised an eyebrow, determined to keep her face straight. 'I'm afraid I don't make house-calls.'

'Not even for friends and neighbours?'

'Not even.'

'You're a hard woman, Grace Allinson. Shall we dance?'

It was a mistake. When she moved in to his arms she was made immediately aware of how very strong the physical pull was between them. He held her too closely, although she tried to tell herself he had to because of lack of space. The floor was quite crowded, and small to begin with, but he was not obliged to hold her the way he was holding her, so that she could feel every inch of him, the hard length of his body against hers.

And then his lips were against her temple and he was speaking softly. 'Perhaps this wasn't such a good idea. I'm having difficulty concentrating.'

She didn't look at him, she knew her face was going pink. 'Maybe you should loosen your hold a little.'

'Why don't we just call it a day, get out of here?'

'If—if you like.'

It was raining when they got outside. They laughed and made a dash for his car, gleaming silver in the lights of the car park. Grace slid in to the passenger seat while he held the door open for her, laughing again as he let out a low whistle, his eyes on her legs.

'By the way, when do I get to see your new horses?'

'Horses!' He switched on the ignition, stuck the gear lever into drive and pulled away smoothly, laughing again. 'How can you think of horses at a time like this?'

A time like what? She wasn't going to voice the question, she knew what he meant, she had been aware of his response to her on the dance-floor. His mind was working very differently from hers and it made her nervous. It was for that reason that she started to chatter. 'Where—I mean, when did you learn to ride?'

'In South America. Ten years ago. I was over there for four months, I took to it like a duck to water.'

'To South America?'

'To riding, you idiot!'

She was laughing again, nervous laughter. What the devil was the matter with her, why did she feel she had to be on guard? Because she felt sure he was going to pounce, that was why, and she wasn't exactly surprised when he pulled off the road, about halfway between the restaurant and their homes. She knew what to expect when he turned into a narrow, deserted lane and cut the engine.

But she was quite wrong. Demetrius made no move, he merely looked at her. She couldn't see his face too well because it was so dark and wet outside and there was no moon, but she could hear the concern plainly in his voice.

'What's the matter, Grace? Why are you suddenly twitchy?'

'I——' She felt foolish. Had it been so obvious? 'I'm not.'

'Then relax.' His hand came out and slid under her hair at the nape. 'You're tense, I can feel it.' His fingers started massaging the top of her neck, and it didn't help one bit. It just made things worse. His touch was nothing short of erotic, or so it seemed to her.

'Demetrius——' She turned to him, her eyes beseeching. For what, she wasn't sure.

His hand dropped to her shoulders, and he pulled her swiftly into his arms, his mouth claiming hers

with a pressure which parted her lips and made her
head spin. He kissed her forcefully, deeply, and
although it was what she wanted, had been wanting
all evening, she resisted. 'Demetrius—enough,
please!'

He just laughed, his lips moving to the base of
her ear, to the delicate skin at the side of her neck.
When she shivered at the touch, he laughed again,
soft laughter which was in itself exciting to her.
'Enough, Grace? I've been longing to kiss you all
evening, and you know it. You've felt the same
way.'

'No. I—please.' She heard the note of pleading
in her own voice, and then, annoyed with herself,
she snapped at him. 'Demetrius, let *go* of me.'

He let go of her at once, his black eyes searching
hers. 'Hey, take it easy, will you?'

'I'm sorry, it's just—it's all a bit much,' she said
lamely.

'Could you enlarge upon that for me?'

She had been holding her breath; she let it out
slowly now, on one long sigh. Once again she opted
to keep things simpler by saying precisely what she
was thinking, feeling. 'I mean I'm extremely attracted to you and it comes as a shock, quite
honestly.'

'It does?' There was just the hint of a smile
pulling at the corners of his mouth. 'You mean you
don't want to be?'

'No, I don't mean that. Well, not exactly. I
mean...'

'You mean you need a little time to get used to
the idea?'

She took his offering gratefully. 'Yes, I—think
that's what I'm trying to say.'

There was a momentary silence. Demetrius put a finger to her lips, moving it very slowly as he traced their outline, while Grace sat motionless, with a knot of tension inside her unlike anything she had ever felt before. She couldn't look him in the eyes any longer, she couldn't, because if she did he would see the desire in her own eyes and she did not want things to go any further than they had.

'Is there someone?' he asked softly.

'What? What do you mean?'

'Come on, Grace, I mean is there a man in your life, someone who——'

'No.' It came out on a note of surprise; she thought he had realised that. 'No, there's no one.'

'Then what's wrong?'

She had kept her eyes on his chin, had tried to concentrate on the square, unyielding shape of it. They moved to his mouth now and she quickly dragged them away. 'Nothing's wrong. I just told you—this is all a bit much, a bit fast.'

He considered that, and her, for a long moment. At length, he nodded slightly, firing the engine as he spoke. 'All right, you need time, I'll give you time. But you know what's happening between us, Grace, and I don't see why you should fight against it.'

She was annoyed by that. 'You seem to be taking a lot for granted, Demetrius. I've told you, that's a mistake as far as I'm concerned.'

'We'll see,' he said softly, turning to glance at her. 'We'll see, my lovely.'

They drove back to the manor in silence, both occupied with their thoughts. When he brought the Mercedes to a halt, he turned to her and said he would see her indoors.

'There's no need for that.'

He wagged a finger at her. 'You'll do as you're told, Miss Allinson.'

She shrugged. 'I see you're not called Knight for nothing. OK, if you insist on being gallant...'

He saw her inside, had a look around and pronounced the place safe. 'You don't get spooked, being here alone so much?'

'Matty's in bed upstairs.'

'Ah, that's all right then,' he grinned. 'I'm sure no one would *dare* break in while the buxom Matilda's on the premises!'

Grace was giggling now. 'You have a fine imagination. We're in the peaceful English countryside. You lived in London for too long.'

He caught hold of her by the waist, pulling her against him, grinning. 'Perhaps I did. Look what I've been missing all this time. Why did your father never tell me his daughter was a beauty?'

'A beauty therapist?' she teased, her eyes dancing with laughter. She tried to wriggle away from him but it didn't work, his grasp tightened.

And his smile vanished. 'A beauty,' he said quietly, firmly. 'My God, if you will insist on looking at me like that, with those gorgeous big blue eyes...' Suddenly it was happening again, he was kissing her and, this time, she didn't resist. She kissed him back. Maybe it was because she felt safe now, being on home ground.

Which was stupid of her. She learned, fast, that giving Demetrius Knight the slightest encouragement was a very risky business. He was easily aroused, a passionate man whose mixed European blood was very easily inflamed. He groaned against her mouth, his tongue probing, probing and ex-

citing, his hands sliding to her bottom as he pulled
her hips tightly against his.

'Demetrius——' She had to break away from him
roughly, otherwise she wouldn't have escaped. 'I—
it's time I went to bed.'

He raised an eyebrow. 'There's no answer to
that.'

Grace couldn't laugh, she had to stick to her guns
this time. How could she have thought herself safe
here? Matilda would be aware of nothing, she was
in the wing at the other end of the house.

'Goodnight, Demetrius, and thanks for a lovely
evening.'

'Are you trying to tell me something?'

She laughed in spite of herself then. It was something else she liked about him, his sense of humour.
'If there's one thing I do admire, it's a man who's
quick on the uptake!'

'Hey, seriously now.' He caught hold of her hand,
smiling. 'How about coming for a ride with me in
the morning, bright and early? Can you manage
that? I'll introduce you to Horace and Greta.'

'I'd be delighted! Shall we say six o'clock? I think
that's the nicest part of the day. I'll come to you,
shall I? And I'll introduce you to Annabel.'

He nodded, smiling, bending forward to kiss the
tip of her nose. 'Sounds good to me. But you're
wrong about that, at least as far as today is concerned. I'd say—oh, that somewhere between eight
o'clock and midnight was the nicest part of the day.
Goodnight, Grace.'

'Goodnight, Demetrius.'

She went up to her room feeling light-hearted.
She had enjoyed the evening and she was looking
forward to riding with him in the morning. There

was so much more to him than she had imagined, he was more sensitive than his sister gave him credit for, he was also more...more what, exactly?

Grace woke earlier than she had intended to. It wouldn't take long to get ready, but there was no point in going back to sleep, even if she could. She flung back the bedclothes, eager to get round to Demetrius.

It didn't show on her, the fact that she hadn't had enough sleep. Demetrius was just saddling Horace, a three-year-old chestnut-coloured stallion who did *not* suit his name. Still, Horace it was; he was a magnificent animal, as was his master. Grace's eyes flicked appreciatively over Demetrius in his riding gear, her smile instantly being returned by him, as was her look of appreciation.

'Good morning, Grace. You're looking good. You have an unfair advantage, you know.'

'Over whom?'

'Other women, of course. Not many women look so good this early in the morning.'

She supposed he would know about that, and she told herself to keep a balance on things, not to let this new friendship go to her head. They trotted along the bridle path which cut through the woods and turned left on to Feathers Lane. It was a route Grace knew like the back of her hand. They rode for just under an hour, enjoying the crisp morning air, the solitude, a conversation which was intermittent but comfortable. Demetrius laughed when she told him Horace was ill-named.

'He doesn't look at all like a Horace.'

'Is that so? What does he look like?'

'More like a—oh, I don't know. He needs a stronger name. Speaking of which, what does the "K" stand for?'

'What?'

'In DKK Holdings. What's the middle "K" for?'

'Kester. Sorry about that!' He shrugged. 'It was my father's idea, a tribute to an army buddy of his, someone who was killed in action. It's actually a diminutive of Christopher, but Kester is what I got on my birth certificate.'

'I like it.' She paused, considering what she'd just said. 'Yes, I do...but I'm not sure about it with Demetrius Knight on either side of it!'

'Absolutely, I couldn't agree more.'

She was reluctant to part from him when they had to part, when it was time to go to work. They rode together to the stables at the manor, but Demetrius made no mention of seeing her that night. The extent of her disappointment angered her—hadn't she told herself not to let this thing go to her head, not to read too much into it?

That proved to be difficult, because Demetrius dismounted and reached for her, catching hold of her by the waist and pulling her into his arms. It was minutes before they separated, by which time they were both breathless and Grace was bewildered all over again. To think she had so recently disliked this man, and now...now she was in danger of liking him too much. 'I really must get a move on, Demetrius.'

'Me, too. I'll see you at the weekend, Grace. I'll ring you.'

The weekend. But it was only Thursday today. In any case, she couldn't manage it. 'No, not at the weekend. I want to talk to my father, remember? I want—well, just to be with him.'

Something unreadable flitted across his face. 'He's coming home for the weekend, is he?'

'I assume so, I'm expecting him home tomorrow.' What was this? Why should he suppose her father might not come home? Because he hadn't come home last weekend? 'He doesn't normally stay in London over the weekend.'

'I see. Then I'll see you early next week. I'll ring you to make arrangements.'

'Please do.' She hoped she was managing to hide her pleasure, to appear friendly but not over-enthusiastic. She stood, watching until he was out of sight, knowing that he was going to be on her mind all day whether she liked it or not.

He was, and when his sister telephoned at lunch time that day, Grace cursed herself for her own stupidity.

'Grace?' Melissa sounded fed up and she said as much. 'I'm bored. Can I come round to your house tonight? Only, Demetrius just phoned to tell me he won't be coming home this evening, he's spending the night in London. Honestly, it's all right for *him*. He'd made no mention of this before, but suddenly he tells me he has to go to a party. A likely story! Of course it means he's spending the night with one of his women. He must think I'm . . . oops, sorry, Grace!'

'For what?' Her voice was tight, she could hear it. She was in no doubt that Melissa had jumped to the right conclusion—but why did it hurt? She hadn't supposed for one minute that Demetrius led a celibate life. He had everything going for him; wealth, sophistication, experience, looks—and an apartment in London, an apartment he wasn't going to give up just because he had a place in the country.

'For being tactless. Demetrius is always telling me that tact is not my strongest point. I didn't mean...well, I know he was out with you last night and——'

'And nothing,' Grace put in. 'That was no big deal, don't let your vivid imagination run riot, Melissa.' It was good advice; she should listen to it herself. 'It doesn't mean a thing,' she went on. 'Yes, you can come over this evening, but I warn you now, I'm having a heavy day and I shall want an early night.'

It was a heavy day, one that was spoiled by that phone call. Still, it was as well that she knew where she stood, as well to understand that she was not the only female in Demetrius Knight's life.

The telephone was ringing as she walked through the front door of the manor a few hours later. The housekeeper was on her way to answer it, but Grace told her not to bother. 'That's OK, Matty, I'll get it.' She picked up the receiver, knowing it would not be Demetrius but hoping it was.

'Grace? It's me.'

She sighed inwardly at the familiar tones of Rodney Featherstone's voice. 'Hello, love. What's new?'

'I'll tell you what's new—tickets to that musical I was supposed to take you to—acquired at short notice and therefore at great expense. So don't tell me you can't make it.'

'When?'

'Monday.'

She didn't hesitate. 'I can make it,' she said, putting a smile into her voice. 'I'll look forward to it, Rodney.'

'I wish you meant that,' he said softly.

'But I do! Now, would it make life easier for you if I met you in London?'

'As it happens, no. I won't be in the office on Monday, I'll be out with a client during the afternoon so I'll pick you up.'

They chatted for a while before hanging up, at which point Grace stood, looking at her reflection in the hall mirror. She smiled, feeling satisfied, almost childishly so. What was good for the goose was good for the gander. If Demetrius wanted to take her out on Monday—it was hard luck.

Demetrius did ask her out on Monday. He called her at work at nine that morning—and he did not sound pleased on learning that she wasn't available. 'You have other arrangements? But I thought we'd agreed——'

'We didn't agree anything, Demetrius, just that we'd go out this week.'

'Early this week,' he amended. There was a silence. Grace did nothing to fill it. 'What's wrong with you?' he asked at length, when it was clear she wasn't volunteering any further information about her plans.

'Wrong?' she said casually. 'Nothing at all.'

'Like hell. You're playing games, and I'll tell you now, I don't like it.'

'I don't know what you're talking about, Demetrius.'

She heard the click of his tongue, the impatient release of breath. 'All right, Grace, I've got the message—you don't like being taken for granted.'

That she should feel guilty suddenly was ludi-crous, and yet she did. 'It isn't that,' she said hastily. 'Honestly. It's—I'm going to the theatre with a friend, it was planned some time ago so there's nothing I can do about it. The tickets——'

'You're not going to see the new Stoppard play by any chance?'

'No, I——'

'Good. Because I've got us tickets for that for Wednesday. In the meantime, come and have lunch with me.'

'Today?'

'Of course today.'

'Oh, Demetrius, I can't, I'm sorry.' She *was* sorry, she was longing to see him—whether it was wise or not. 'My appointment book is absolutely full, I'll be lucky if I can grab a sandwich today. I—how about tomorrow?'

'I can't manage lunch.' There was a smile in his voice when he went on, much to her relief, 'So I'll pick you up for dinner. Eight o'clock.'

'Eight o'clock tomorrow,' she said. 'I'll look forward to it.'

When she put the receiver down, her eyes closed of their own accord. Something told her she was fighting a losing battle, that, much as she wished to play it cool with Demetrius, she wasn't going to succeed. The idea of seeing Rodney tonight did nothing for her, whereas tomorrow—tomorrow, she knew, she would be feeling very differently...

CHAPTER SIX

'BUT it's such a long drive back to Windsor!'
Rodney complained, reaching for her in the con-
fines of his sports car. Grace's dates with him always
ended with a kiss, but there was nothing exciting
about them. In a way, she regarded Rodney like a
brother; he had known Thomas for years and had
at one time been a regular houseguest at the manor.

'Don't be ridiculous, Rodney, it's twenty minutes
down the motorway.' She was laughing at him, he
had just invited himself in for a cup of coffee and,
while this was nothing unusual, she wasn't in the
mood tonight. He would keep her up, talking, about
his work in advertising in the West End, about
his social life, his family. The Featherstone family all
lived in Windsor, Rodney in a small bachelor pad
not far from the family home—but far enough so
he was guaranteed privacy.

Grace had enjoyed her evening with him, as she
always did, but Demetrius had been constantly in
the back of her mind even while she'd been
watching the musical—not very far back, either.

'There's something different about you tonight,
Grace.' It wasn't the first time Rodney had said it,
but he wasn't laughing this time, he wasn't teasing
her, he was asking her to explain. 'Why is that?
What gives?'

'Just because I'm not inviting you in, you mean?'

He shook his head, his thick sandy hair shifting
across his forehead. He was grinning. 'Don't play

cat and mouse with me, I know you too well. You're
a woman with a secret. Share it with me.'

A secret? She looked at him blankly, wondering
in what way he perceived her as different. If Rodney
had his way, they would see a lot more of each
other; her feelings towards him might be sisterly,
but his feelings towards her had changed some years
ago. Whereas once she had been regarded as the
pesky younger sister of his friend Thomas, when
Grace had moved back to Allinson Manor after her
training, after the Raymond Ferris episode, Rodney
had changed towards her. After having been absent
from his orbit for a couple of years, he had then
begun to see her as a woman, an attractive and
interesting woman.

'What have you been up to since I last saw you?'
he persisted. 'Now let me guess . . . you're thinking
of opening another branch of The Beauty Parlour?
Or two?'

With a shake of her head, she smiled at him. He
would think in those terms; he was ambitious in
his own career and seemed to think Grace more
ambitious than she actually was. Indeed, the continued success of her business had lost some of its
importance to her now, now she had proved herself,
to herself and to her father, now she had had his
acknowledgement, now they were friends again. She
enjoyed it, always had and always would because
she believed in what she was doing, the service she
provided, but it had suddenly ceased to be the ob-
session it used to be.

'No. And I haven't been up to anything at all,'
she said firmly. 'Now give me a kiss and get moving,
you villain. You're not coming in for coffee be-

cause you'll keep me talking half the night and I'm tired.'

It was Demetrius she was thinking of as Rodney kissed her goodnight, him with whom she was comparing Rodney. Even the lightest touch from his lips was enough to inflame her—while Rodney's kiss did nothing to her. Why was it that one man's kiss could send the blood storming through her veins, while another's left her cold?

Kissing Rodney might have left her cold, but it had quite a different effect on him. 'Grace?' He put a hand to her cheek, turning her face in an effort to look in to her eyes. 'You've never kissed me like that before. I have to say, I like it!'

She felt awful, guilty. She had kissed him back while thinking of another man—and she had known very well what she was doing. Of course she had. She had been . . . experimenting, in a way, trying to see whether, if she put a little more effort into it, she could respond to Rodney's kisses the way she responded to Demetrius'. There was a part of her which did not want to feel the way she felt when she was in Demetrius' arms; discovering how strongly she was attracted to him was something she hadn't adjusted to.

Now Rodney was reaching for her again, and she had to get away from him. Encouraging him, albeit unwittingly, was unfair. 'I must go, love.' She opened the passenger door quickly, startling him. 'Sorry, but I really am whacked.'

'Wait a minute!' He got out of the car and caught up with her. 'Will I see you this weekend? It's Easter and I thought——'

'No. I'm committed. I told you, Daddy's bringing his girlfriend to meet me and Thomas.

She'll be here all weekend and I feel I should stick around.'

He nodded, a reluctant but accepting gesture. 'I suppose so. What day is Thomas coming home?'

'Thursday.'

He nodded again, shrugging. 'All right. I'll be in touch.'

Grace made her escape, thinking she should stop seeing Rodney altogether. In a way, she had used him tonight, she disliked herself for that; she had wanted simply to be unavailable to Demetrius, to show him she was not at his beck and call, to be taken out only when it suited him...but she had learned that there was no escaping Demetrius Knight. When she wasn't with him, she was thinking about him just the same.

Thoughts of him kept her awake, anticipating tomorrow evening, until at length she grew impatient with herself. Not since Raymond Ferris had any man occupied her thoughts so much. Apart from Rodney there had been no one in her life since Raymond, no one, nothing except her business, only the odd night out with a girlfriend who lived in Reading, an ex-school friend. Oh, there had been the occasional date as well, certainly, but no one she had wanted to see on a regular basis...until Demetrius.

She glanced at the clock on her bedside table, counting the hours till she would see him. Counting the hours and wondering why he had had such an impact on her in so short a time.

'And how was your evening at the theatre?' It was the first thing Demetrius asked her the following evening when he picked her up.

'Super, thank you.'

'You didn't mention who you were going with,' he said, as he handed her into the passenger seat of his car. Fortunately he didn't wait for her response, but closed the door and walked round to the driver's seat. It gave Grace a few seconds in which to think. Until this moment, she had every intention of telling him who she had been out with. Why shouldn't she?

Why shouldn't she? she asked herself again, as she struggled with her feelings. On the one hand, she wanted very much to tell him who she had been out with, but on the other hand ... something was warning her not to mention Rodney's name. Unable to pinpoint the reason for this, she told herself she simply didn't want to risk spoiling the evening.

'Grace? I was saying, you didn't mention who you were going to the theatre with.'

'Oh, just a friend,' she said casually, reaching to smooth back her hair. She had left it loose tonight, because Demetrius had told her he preferred it that way.

Her action did not go unnoticed, in spite of his driving the car. 'Very nice, too. And you're wearing that delicious perfume.'

Inwardly, she breathed a sigh of relief. The subject of her night out didn't get mentioned again. As they drove to the restaurant, they talked generalities for a while—until Demetrius asked her how her weekend with her father had gone.

'I'll tell you about it later,' she said. She had asked Demetrius to take her to the restaurant they had been to the previous week, and she waited until they were settled, until they had been served with cocktails and had ordered their meal. 'The weekend

went beautifully,' she said then, 'and Daddy told
me all about Phyllis Radcliffe. He's bringing her
to your housewarming party,' she added, before realising that Demetrius probably knew this already.
She picked up her cocktail, raised the glass in the
air and smiled. 'Here's to my father and his lady-
friend, then.'

Demetrius drank the toast, but he cautioned her
not to be premature. 'She's a charming woman
but—well, don't make too much of it at this stage.'

'So you have met her.'

'Yes. I couldn't say anything to you before, you
do see that? Your father specifically asked me not
to.'

Grace saw a lot of things; she could work out
the rest, the little details she hadn't actually been
told by anyone. Demetrius had met Phyllis
Radcliffe, Councillor Mrs Radcliffe, with whom Sir
Nigel was involved in London, but he had been
unable to mention the fact to Grace. According to
her father, Mrs Radcliffe was a widow, fifty-two
years old and not just charming, but *very* charming.

Grace knew, now, why her father hadn't mentioned Mrs Radcliffe's existence. She had had a very
successful weekend with him and they had, at her
instigation, talked about the past.

Sir Nigel had been obviously relieved, pleased.
'I've always felt you'd never forgiven me,' he'd said,
'even though you knew Raymond Ferris was just
a golddigger.'

'Just a golddigger.' Grace had repeated the
words. 'Yes, he was no more than that. But you
were right, I hadn't forgiven you, I see that now,
though I believed I had. Oh, I realised long since
that you only did what was best for me but—well,

I think I've resented your daring to interfere. I thought I was perfectly grown up and should have been allowed to do what I wanted, which serves nicely to demonstrate how very immature I was, since I was going to marry Raymond!'

'Quite.'

Grace smiled. 'You're forgiven, Daddy, I want you to know that. Resenting the past had become a habit with me, just as we've got into the habit of not communicating with one another. It was only when I was talking to Demetrius that I realised...' She had gone on to put him fully in the picture about their neighbours, had told him everything there was to tell. Well, almost everything...

It had been on the Sunday that Sir Nigel mentioned Mrs Radcliffe. It had provoked another lengthy talk, which had been a good thing, had brought them even closer.

Grace had admonished her father, gently. 'It was silly of you not to tell me. I suspected, in any case. She even answered the phone once when I called you in London. I can't say you're good at keeping your women secret!'

But her father hadn't laughed, he had looked sheepish, more like a schoolboy than the powerful man he was. 'I didn't know how you'd react, Grace.'

'What does that mean?'

'Well, your mother...it's less than four years since she died.'

Grace's heart went out to him. She felt tears spring to her eyes and did nothing to prevent them. It was, just less than four years, but four years was a long time. She said as much. It was difficult to say more, difficult actually to voice what she was

thinking, because her voice seemed to have deserted her. How lonely her father must have been
all that time! He had been devoted to her mother,
they had been devoted to one another. Her death
had brought about a reconciliation between Grace
and her father, but it had been only a partial reconciliation. Until now. She had moved back into
the manor with him—but in many ways they had
been strangers. His son had been away at
Cambridge all that time and...yes, her father must
have been lonely, must have missed his wife terribly.

'Oh, Daddy!' Grace's voice had cracked at that
point. She went over to him and put her arms
around him. 'Life's too short, isn't it, for all these
misunderstandings and complications?'

'Yes,' he said quietly. 'It is.'

'Bring your lady here to meet me, Daddy. You'll
see how I react, you goose! I shall welcome her
with open arms.'

'Hey! Now don't start imagining wedding bells,
it's early days yet!'

They had laughed then. Together. For the first
time in a long time.

Grace shared it all with Demetrius over dinner;
she told him of her conversations with her father
because she felt close enough to him to be able to
do so. He appreciated it, too, she could tell.

'So he's bringing Phyllis to the party.' He was
smiling.

'She's spending the weekend with us, arriving on
Good Friday.' And the party was on Saturday.
Melissa was catering for it, from choice. Demetrius
had offered to bring professional caterers in, but
she had declined because she wanted to do it herself
and she was excited about it.

'Your father can kill two birds with one stone, so to speak. Your brother Thomas is definitely coming home, isn't he?'

'Yes, I spoke to him on the phone today, actually. He was delighted at the idea of Daddy having a girlfriend. He will be coming to the party, by the way.'

Demetrius nodded, glancing around. 'If I'd known the trio weren't playing here tonight, I'd have taken you somewhere else.' He turned back to look at her closely then, as if her response was important. 'Why did you want to come back here, Grace?'

'Because we enjoyed it so much last week, I told you it's one of my favourite——'

'I know what you told me,' he cut in quietly, his eyes fixed on hers, 'but I wonder whether there's more to it than that.'

'I don't know what you mean.' Nor did she. Was he really put out because there was no live music tonight? She shrugged, grinning mischievously. 'What's the matter, do you think I'm avoiding dancing with you or something?'

She meant it as a joke, but it did not have the desired effect. He leaned closer to her, suddenly very serious. 'I'll tell you what I think—or rather, what I suspect. You've just told me what you said to Nigel—that resenting the past had become a habit with you.'

'Yes?'

'And Nigel told me there's been no serious boyfriend in your life since Raymond Ferris.'

'So? I don't know what you're getting at.'

In a rare, typically continental gesture, he spread his hands, palms up, fingers splayed. 'Think about

it, about all of that. To what extent has your past,
your experience with Ferris, affected you?'

Grace was still at a loss. 'I'm sorry, you'll have
to be more explicit.'

He was. 'Right, referring to your earlier
question—yes, I think you're avoiding me in all
sorts of ways. You've refused more dates than
you've accepted from me, you keep telling me not
to take you for granted, and I think you wanted to
come here tonight because this restaurant is out of
the way. Because you're not likely to be seen by
people you know—seen with me.'

'Demetrius——'

'Let me finish,' he said, as if she had any choice.
'I think you're afraid to acknowledge what's happening between us, I think you want to keep a low
profile on this relationship, because you're afraid.'

He had finally finished—but Grace was unable
to respond for a full minute. She was speechless;
she wasn't angry, she was confused. 'I swear I don't
know what you're talking about! To start with,
what have I got to be afraid of?'

'You tell me,' he said evenly, his eyes not leaving
hers. 'Being hurt? Commitment? Another affair
that might turn sour—albeit for different reasons.'

Another affair? Her mind went into overdrive.
Firstly, she had never had an *affair* with Raymond,
secondly——'My God!' she exclaimed, as anger
made itself known. 'You really do take a lot for
granted! If you have in mind an affair——'

'Oh, come on, Grace! Where else do you think
we're heading?'

What happened to her in the ensuing minutes was
strange. Her anger died as quickly as it had flared
up. His question had been fair enough. Of course

he was making assumptions, he knew how strongly she was attracted to him and—well, no doubt affairs were a way of life for him. It wasn't so for her. But he didn't know that, so she could hardly be angry with him. She was, after all, twenty-four years old, a successful businesswoman who was apparently sophisticated and experienced...

'Grace? Where have you gone?'

'I'm—I was just thinking.' She lifted her head, an unconscious gesture of determination. The evening was not going to be spoiled, she wasn't going to allow that to happen. Demetrius was looking at her, expecting a reasonable answer to what he saw as a reasonable question. 'I don't know,' she said softly, 'I really don't know where we're heading. But this much I can tell you, as far as I'm concerned we're friends. I didn't plan it,' she added, smiling, 'it just happened. So why don't we just wait and see what else happens?'

Later, much later, as she lay alone in her bed, she wished she had been more assertive, she wished she had told him that he had a nerve if he thought he was lining her up to be his next mistress—or one of several current ones.

For the moment, however, she said no more, because Demetrius' next words robbed her of speech once again. He inclined his head, considering her, his smile slow and wickedly attractive. 'No, Grace, I'll tell you what's going to happen. Sooner or later you and I are going to make love and it will be unlike anything you've ever experienced before. That's the kind of chemistry we have buzzing between us, and don't bother to deny it. As for the immediate future—tomorrow you will dress up to the nines,' he told her, 'and I shall wine you and dine you in London after the theatre. I shall show you off to as many people as I can. Do you understand me?'

She understood him all right. In spite of herself, his words brought a flush of pleasure to her cheeks. She didn't know about the first part of his threat . . . or promise . . . she knew only that she felt happier than she had felt in many years.

When they got back to the manor, he took the front-door key from her and looked around, flicking light switches. 'All's well. Right, who's going to make the coffee?'

Grace was looking at her watch, shaking her head. Tomorrow was a working day. 'I'm tired, Demetrius, I don't think——'

He advanced on her, telling her he wasn't interested in what she thought. Laughing, she retreated, both hands held up in front of her. 'Well, that's charming! You're not int——'

He wasn't put off, he never was. She was encircled in his arms right there in the hall, before she could finish what she'd been saying, and when his mouth came down on hers she forgot her protest, she was aware only of the masculine scent of him, of the feel of his body, so tall and solid against her own. His lips moved from her mouth to the side of her neck, the place he had discovered to be her weakness, and it was all she could do not to moan her pleasure aloud. Checking her response to him was almost impossible, yet she didn't dare encourage him further.

When at last he spoke her name, it was in a voice thick with desire. 'Grace——'

'Please, don't say it.' She seized her chance and stepped smartly backwards, away from him. He didn't need to say it, she knew he wanted her, right now. 'I'll—I'll put the kettle on.'

His eyes narrowed, searching hers as if searching for information. 'Forget it,' he said, but not impatiently. 'I said I'd give you time, and you want to hold me to that, don't you?'

Grace chose her words with care, knowing he was a man of his word. 'Yes, I want you to honour that promise, Demetrius.'

There was a momentary silence, during which he smiled appreciatively; he knew how clever she thought she was being. 'Very well,' he said quietly. Then his hand snaked out and caught hold of her chin, raising her face, obliging her to look at him. His eyes were glittering darkly, without any trace of humour now. 'But you'll remember what I said to you earlier. And remember something else: I'm going to take you out just as often as I can, here, there and everywhere, so I don't want any more reticence in that department. And there's one more thing, my lovely—don't play games with me, I've already warned you about that.'

It was because of those words that she found herself lying awake in bed again, wishing she had been more assertive. What was the matter with her? Why did she allow herself to be dictated to by him? She had known all along that Demetrius was the domineering type, but—what magic did he wield that made her not mind this? Perhaps it was stupid, but coming from him it made her feel feminine. He was so different from the other men she knew, vastly different from Raymond, of course, and—well, just different altogether.

He had surprised her all over again tonight. One thing was for sure, the more she learned about him,

the more interesting he became to her. Perhaps too
much so. She had to watch it. The last thing she
wanted was to fall in love with him, that would
make it an entirely different ball-game—too
dangerous by half. She went to sleep, eventually,
with that thought firmly in her mind.

It seemed perverse that she should wake at five
the following morning. She looked at the clock and
groaned. Why this, when she was so short of sleep?
How could she be feeling so rested, so *alive*, at this
ungodly hour?

She flung the bedclothes back. There was only
one thing for it, she would get up and take some
exercise. Annabel would be glad of it.

Annabel was glad of it—and so was Horace. She
spotted Demetrius on the bridle path and caught
up with him. He seemed as surprised as she that
she was up and about. 'Well! Good morning, my
beauty! Just a minute—aren't you the woman who
protested she was too tired to make coffee last
night?'

'The very same.' She laughed even as she shook
her head. 'Blame it on springtime or something—
I don't know, I'm just full of beans this morning.'

'I hope it lasts,' Demetrius said wryly. 'Because
there's no way, and I mean no way, we're going to
cut short our date tonight.'

It didn't occur to her to try. When he came for
her that evening she was dressed up to the nines,
as per instructions, and eager to go.

His eyes moved slowly over her as he greeted her.
'Fabulous! Black velvet is very sexy, it suits you.
And it will set this off nicely.' To Grace's aston-
ishment he handed her a small, dark blue jewellery
box. In it was a gold chain, beautiful in its sim-

plicity. She looked at it, not knowing what to say, and then she saw how intricately plaited its links were. It felt heavy and cool in her hand; it was solid gold and it was very expensive, of that she was sure.

'I—Demetrius, I can't accept a gift like this!'

'Of course you can, it's just a little token of appreciation. Now come here.' He took the chain from her, telling her to hold up her hair while he fastened it in place. He stood behind her, then he turned her around to face him and he hooked his fingers under the chain, pulling her forward so he could kiss her. 'You're wearing that perfume again.'

'But of course, it's my favourite.'

'That makes two of us. Come on, let's get this show on the road.'

He seemed unable to take his eyes off her, and as they drove into the West End she teased him at regular intervals about keeping his eyes on the traffic.

'I'd much rather look at you,' he told her. 'What *is* that perfume? No, don't tell me. I shall simply think of it as you.' He was looking at her again. 'Should I catch a whiff of it anywhere else, I shall think of you—and in particular our very first meeting. I shall be haunted.'

Grace hooted at that. 'A pity.'

'A *pity*? Explain yourself, woman!'

'A pity that you'll have an unpleasant association.'

'Who says it's unpleasant? Just because you weren't on your best behaviour that day, it doesn't mean——'

'Do you mind?' She was indignant. '*I* wasn't on my best behaviour? What about *you*?'

'Why, Grace! Whatever do you mean? I was being my usual charming self.'

'Humph. You might well laugh—and will you *please* keep your eyes on the road?'

The evening continued in a jocular vein. Tom Stoppard's play was hilarious and Grace loved it. Surreptitiously, she glanced often at Demetrius, gratified to see him enjoying himself so much. Time and again her hand moved to feel the chain at her neck; she was touched by his generosity, and curious about it. Discoveries, she was making discoveries about him every time she saw him, about his character, his sense of humour, sense of mischief, his likes and his dislikes.

They discussed in detail the play they had seen while they dined that evening—and no sooner were they headed for home than Demetrius was talking about their being together the next night. More than anything Grace wanted to say yes, but she couldn't. She explained about her brother coming home. 'I want to have a natter with him alone. I see so little of Thomas, I'm looking forward to spending the evening with him, before my father and Mrs Radcliffe descend.'

Demetrius' answer was a long time in coming. 'Are you telling me I won't see you on Friday, either?'

'Well . . . yes. I'm—I'll have to be at the manor, surely you can understand that?'

He merely grunted, his eyes firmly on the road at that point.

'Besides,' she went on, 'it doesn't seem right to leave Melissa alone night after night.'

This time, there wasn't even as much as a grunt. She glanced at him worriedly. 'Demetrius?'

'My sister,' he said at length, 'is perfectly able to entertain herself—the fact that she's housebound is entirely her own fault, remember.'

'Yes, I remember. By the way, has she said any more about going to college?'

'She said, and I quote, that she has it in hand, whatever that means.'

Grace turned to look out of the window, frowning. 'I hope she hasn't changed her mind.'

'So do I. Knowing her, she might well. But it's not your problem, Grace, and I won't have you worrying about it.'

The remark pleased her, it made her feel that he wanted to protect her. 'I shan't. She'll sort herself out, as I did when I was her age.'

When they got inside the manor, Demetrius surprised her yet again. He saw that she was safe, but that was all, he made no attempt to kiss her, to touch her in any way. 'Goodnight, Grace.'

'Demetrius!' She was staring at his back, he was opening the front door—leaving at once. 'What is it? What's wrong? Please tell me...' But she already knew. His mood had changed on the way home, when Melissa had been mentioned. Why? Why did he continue to be cross with his young sister? And he was, she remembered the tightening of his expression when she had first mentioned Melissa's name. She had the feeling there were things she didn't know, that as much as Melissa had told her about herself, there was more. She knew also that, whatever it was, Demetrius wouldn't tell her, he wouldn't talk about his sister in her absence, it wasn't his style. 'It's what I said about Melissa, isn't it? I was only thinking——'

'It has nothing to do with her. It's you.'

'Me?' She moved closer to him. 'What have I done? What have I said?'

'It's your attitude, Grace. Why avoid me just because your family's coming home?'

'Avoid—I'm not avoiding you! Please don't think that!'

'What am I supposed to think? I thought I'd made my point, but you still seem determined to keep a low profile on our—friendship, as you call it.'

'You're wrong,' she told him, repeating it firmly. 'I'd shout about it from the rooftops if you asked me to.'

For long moments he was silent, looking deeply into her eyes. Then, much to her relief, he laughed. 'That won't be necessary. Come for a ride with me in the mornings and I'll make do with that.'

'Done,' she said. 'Furthermore, I'll let everyone know about it, all right? Does that make you happy?'

'Happy?' He pretended to think about it, his eyes dancing with laughter now. 'I don't know. From now until morning is a long time. I need a little comfort, a little something to keep me going.'

Grace looked him in the eye, her own eyes big and innocent. 'Oh. Sorry, but I can't think of anything.'

'Is that a fact?' He was laughing openly, telling her she lacked imagination. 'Perhaps you need a little coaxing.'

'Coaxing? Or did you say coaching?'

'Oh, no, my lovely. I said nothing about coaching, that's one thing you don't need.'

That was what he thought! Nevertheless, she moved willingly into his arms and gave him what comfort she was prepared to give.

CHAPTER SEVEN

'MY DAUGHTER'S at Cambridge.' Mrs Radcliffe was looking at Thomas. It was Good Friday and they were all in the dining-room, enjoying the conversation and the superb meal Matty had produced.

'Really? I didn't know.' Thomas looked at her over the top of his spectacles. It was a gesture so like his father's that Grace couldn't help smiling. Apart from that, however, the two men were like chalk and cheese. Thomas was tall and thin, an intensely serious man, one who dressed purely to keep himself warm, without a thought for his appearance, and who was happiest when he was in a laboratory.

It was good to have him home, good that they were all together again. All? Grace looked at Phyllis Radcliffe with approval. The woman was slender and impeccable, seeming younger than her years. Her hair was dark brown and, if it had been rinsed, it was the most natural-looking colour. She was also diplomatic, a good conversationalist. 'She's studying medicine,' she was saying. 'I don't know where this trait has come from, because there are no other medics in my family, or in that of my late husband, but my son is a doctor and now Sally is well on the way. Still, as long as they're both happy...that's all one can ask for one's children. Nigel, this fish is delicious, I really must compliment your housekeeper. Matilda, isn't it?'

Grace answered before her father could. He had his mouth full. 'Yes, it's Matilda. We call her Matty. She's a gem, she's been with us for years and years.'

'Since the week before I was born,' Thomas put in, being precise, as was his wont. 'That's twenty-seven years, five months and two weeks.'

'And two weeks?' Phyllis twinkled at him, but her teasing went unnoticed. Thomas never noticed when he was being teased.

'And how many days, Thomas?' Grace asked.

'Er—three,' came the serious reply.

She laughed at him. Much as she was enjoying the company, her thoughts kept flitting elsewhere. It had begun well and had continued like that...but after separating from Demetrius this morning the extra sparkle had gone out of it. She was waiting for tomorrow morning, when she would see him again. During the afternoon, she was going next door to help Melissa with the final touches for the party. It was going to be a long day and she could hardly wait for it.

She was up and out with the crack of dawn, getting back to the manor in time for breakfast, wearing jeans and a sweater, no make-up, her black hair tied back in a pony-tail. Phyllis and Sir Nigel were just finishing breakfast and announced that they were going out for a drive.

'Nigel's going to let me drive the Bentley,' Phyllis informed Grace, looking very pleased with herself. 'I don't expect we'll be back before lunch.'

'Well! You *are* honoured.' Grace was impressed. It must be love, she thought, her father had never allowed *her* to drive his car!

Thomas came in as the older two went out. 'What's Dad looking so smug about?'

'I think our father is in love.'

He snorted. 'Don't be daft, Grace. You don't fall in love at that age.'

'Who says? And what would you know?'

Thomas looked hurt. 'What's that supposed to mean?'

'It means, it's never happened to you, so you don't know what it feels like. Age has nothing to do with it.'

She regretted her words. Thomas looked down at the table, started fiddling with a spoon. 'As a matter of fact, it has happened to me.'

He said it so quietly his sister almost didn't catch the words. He looked down in the mouth, so much so that she was at a loss. 'It has? And it went wrong?'

'It's going wrong,' he said, in the same tone of voice. 'She's married.'

'Oh, hell! Oh, Thomas, I—you idiot. How did you allow yourself to get involved with someone who's married?'

'I'm not involved. I—she's on a Master's course and—I see her almost every day. She has no idea how I feel.'

Grace could have wept. So it had happened at long last. Here he was, twenty-seven years of age and loving someone from afar, having what she hoped was no more than a crush on a married woman. She changed the subject at once, deeming it the best thing to do. 'What are your plans for today? You are coming to the party tonight?'

'Yes. I'm looking forward to meeting your new neighbours. In the meantime I'm driving over to Windsor. I'm having lunch with Rodney.'

'Oh!' Grace had banked on having Thomas' company herself till lunch was over. It was only natural he would want to see Rodney, though. It would leave her at a loose end for a couple of hours; perhaps she would go next door earlier than she'd planned to.

Around eleven she telephoned Melissa and suggested it.

'The sooner the better!' Melissa was relieved. 'I fear I've bitten off more than I can chew. How are you at making vol-au-vents and arranging flowers?'

Demetrius was out. Grace was greeted with the news that he was in his office. 'I mean, in Bracknell,' Melissa said. 'Some emergency or something, I don't know anything about it.'

'Oh, well. As long as he's back for tonight.' Grace looked around the kitchen, she saw instantly that Melissa had things well under way. 'You seem very organised, actually.'

They worked, saying little, saying nothing about anything other than what they were doing. There was going to be everything, from champagne and caviar right through to a mind-boggling selection of sweet dishes. Only the ice-cream and gateaux had been bought, Melissa was preparing everything else herself and Grace couldn't help but admire her efforts.

Phyllis Radcliffe, Sir Nigel and Thomas were just finishing tea when Grace got back to the manor. She had the last cup in the pot and sat chatting for a while, grateful to have the weight off her feet. A

0

hot bath, a thorough shampooing of her hair and she would be recharged.

The dress she planned on wearing for the party was new and, a couple of hours later, she looked at it on its hanger and had second thoughts. It was in a deep shade of red, made from a silky, slinky material, and there really wasn't much of it. It had a deep V back and front, narrow shoulder straps and a full, standard length skirt which swished around her legs when she walked. It was the neckline that was worrying her now.

She tried it on to see how she looked now she was made-up, groomed to her usual high standard. Turning through all angles, she looked in the full-length mirror, dubious. While the neckline did more than hint at the swell of her breasts, it didn't actually show anything. Did it?

In search of a second opinion, she went to her brother's room. 'Thomas? May I come in? How do I look?'

He glanced up from the book he was reading. A textbook, typical reading matter for him—pre-party or not! 'Fine.'

'Thomas! Will you kindly *look* at me? At this dress, more specifically.'

He took his glasses off, surveyed her, put them back on again and nodded. 'It's gorgeous, Sis.'

'Really? You don't think it shows too much?'

'Too much what?'

'Boobs, brother dear. Boobs!'

'Oh. No. Honestly.'

'You're sure?' She was thinking she should ask someone else. Mrs Radcliffe, perhaps? But Thomas reassured her, took her seriously and gave the matter careful consideration.

'Now listen, Grace, you don't think I would give my seal of approval if you looked anything less than respectable, do you?'

'No. Er—is that what you're wearing?'

'What's wrong with it?' He was wearing brown cords, a mustard-coloured shirt and one of his jumpers. Grace called them his nineteen-forties jumpers; it was one of those sleeveless, patterned efforts with a shallow V-neck and ribbing.

'Nothing,' she said, smiling. For him, it was right. Thomas didn't possess a suit, or even a regular pair of trousers. 'See you soon. We'll go at around eight, OK?'

'You go when you like. I'll trundle along later, when things have got going a bit.'

Grace retreated. What he meant was, when he'd finished reading. He would put in an appearance only for an hour or so, and then he'd vanish because he'd be bored.

Sir Nigel and Phyllis didn't leave with Grace, either. They, too, said they'd go next door at around nine. Grace got there at a little after eight, and was surprised to see so many people there already. She slipped in the back way, glancing round the kitchen and the dining-room, where the buffet was laid out and looking splendid. She had made a very good job of the flower arrangements, even if she said it herself.

'Grace!' Melissa appeared in the doorway. 'It looks all right, doesn't it?'

'It looks super—and so do you.' Melissa was wearing one of her typically colourful outfits, multi-coloured, in fact; harem pants and a top Grace hadn't seen before.

People were mingling in the sitting-room, drinking, chatting in groups. There were about thirty of them already. Demetrius immediately detached himself from his group and came to Grace, taking her arm. His eyes moved very, very slowly over her, lighting up appreciatively. At her throat she wore the gold chain he had given her, which made him smile. 'Gorgeous! You look beautiful, Grace. Although I think you're being a little unfair...' His eyes were on her cleavage now, making her feel self-conscious all over again, yet inwardly she was amused. He really couldn't take his eyes off her.

It wasn't easy for her to take her eyes off him, either. In a cream-coloured jacket, black trousers and a very fine polo-necked sweater, also black, he looked striking. The short, crisp curls of his hair, thick and coal black, were enough, quite apart from anything else, to make anyone look twice. 'Come on,' he said, 'let me introduce you to my friends and associates. I want to show you off.' He caught hold of her hand and tucked it through his arm. 'But first, let me get you a drink.'

By ten o'clock Grace was on her third drink. She was sticking to Martini and lemonade, because she could handle that without going over the top. Others were less cautious. Nobody was drunk, but the volume of conversation was astonishingly loud and the sitting-room was packed. Altogether there had to be a hundred people present. Some were standing, some sitting, they were scattered in all the downstairs rooms except for Demetrius' office, which was locked, and several couples were dancing on the carpeted area by the swimming pool—Grace's father and Phyllis included.

Demetrius was too busy to give his attention exclusively to Grace, he was pouring drinks and generally being a good host, talking to people, most of whom were, or had been, strangers to her. From time to time she glanced over to the corner of the sitting-room, where Melissa was deep in conversation with Thomas. Seeing them with their heads together surprised her; she couldn't imagine what the two of them had found to talk about. A less likely pairing off than Melissa and Thomas, she could not imagine.

It was getting on for eleven when Rodney Featherstone turned up. Grace was taken aback. The first she knew of his presence was when a pair of arms slid around her waist from the back. She turned, smiling, fully expecting to see Demetrius.

'Rodney! What are you doing here?'

'A nice greeting, I must say!' He laughed. There was the smell of whisky on his breath and she assumed he had begun his evening at some other do. 'You make me sound like a gate-crasher.'

But he was. He hadn't been invited, he hadn't even met Demetrius or his sister. Before anything else could be said, he spotted Thomas and Melissa, caught hold of Grace's hand and set off in their direction.

'You made it, then?' Thomas got up, introducing him to Melissa, who looked him over with open interest. 'How do you do, Rodney?'

There was no interest in Rodney's eyes, he was surveying Grace as closely as Demetrius had when she first arrived. His hand tightened around hers in a quick squeeze as he acknowledged Melissa with nothing more than politeness, extending his free hand. Grace felt him sway slightly. 'Nice to know you, Melissa. I hope you don't mind my dropping in?'

'Of course not!' She smiled prettily, and Thomas looked at her quickly.

'I invited Rodney,' he said. 'He's an old friend of mine. He's been out elsewhere this evening, but I asked him to drop in if he could.'

'I'm delighted,' Melissa said warmly. 'Now, what will you have to drink, Rodney?'

Grace had the feeling he'd had enough to drink already. 'Have you driven here?'

'Got dropped off,' he said, in a voice which sounded normal enough. 'Don't worry, lovely, I shan't be driving home. Thomas suggested I stay over at your place if I made it here.' His hand slid to her waist just as she heard Demetrius' voice behind her. It was as cold as ice.

'Perhaps you'll introduce me, Grace?'

She turned, flushing, aware of his annoyance at what he could see—Rodney's hold on her was nothing short of proprietorial, and she resented it. She could hardly pull away, though, he was an old friend and his feelings would be hurt.

The following few minutes were awkward in the extreme as far as she was concerned. If Melissa were aware of her brother's annoyance, she didn't show it; she introduced the two men and said something about getting drinks.

'I was just saying to your sister,' Rodney said amiably, unaware of any awkwardness, 'I hope you don't mind my dropping in. Old Thomas here— he said you wouldn't mind.'

Demetrius made no response. He turned to his sister. 'Don't bother, Melissa. I'll see to the drinks.'

'I'll give you a hand,' Grace said quickly. 'I need a refill, anyway.' She walked over to the bar in the living-room, a pace behind Demetrius, leaving the other three in the corner. 'I'm sorry about that,' she said hastily. 'I had no idea Rodney was coming, my brother invited him and he probably thought——'

'He seems very fond of you.' Demetrius' eyes had darkened. 'What's the score?'

'I'm—not sure what you mean.'

'I mean,' he said slowly, 'I would like to know exactly what your relationship with him is.'

'Rodney is an old friend—of mine and of Thomas. I've known him for years. We go out together from——' The words were said before she could think about them.

'You *what*?'

'Used to,' she put in quickly. 'We used to go out together from time to time.'

'I thought you told me there was no man in your life?' His voice had an iron edge to it now.

'There isn't.' She forced a laugh and put a hand on his arm. 'Rodney doesn't count, we're just friends. I've told you, he's——'

Demetrius shook his arm free, his eyes black, glowering. 'Friends?' he demanded. '*Just* friends? He was almost salivating at the sight of you! Whose benefit was that dress for, Grace? Mine or his?'

Anger shot through her. She had told him she'd had no idea Rodney was coming and, worse, she didn't like the implications of his thinking the dress was for his benefit, either. If only he knew how she'd almost discarded it, how she'd nearly worn something else, and he was implying now that she'd worn it as a come-on. 'The dress is for *my* benefit,

Demetrius. It happens to be my colour and it happens to be appropriate for a party.'

He was by no means convinced. 'There's something you should know about me,' he said, his eyes riveted on hers. 'I don't like deceit, in women or in men. So I suggest you explain yourself. What do you mean when you say you and that character go out together?'

It took the wind out of her sails; it was true she had never mentioned seeing Rodney but—but deceit was surely too strong a word. She strove for patience, people were looking at them. 'For heaven's sake, I'm deceiving no one. Rodney and I are old friends and we go out—used to go out— occasionally. And that's all there is to it.'

'So when did you last see him? Have you been out with him recently?'

She sighed. Faced with the direct question, she wasn't going to lie. She had done enough hedging, enough placating. She looked at Demetrius levelly. 'Yes, as a matter of fact. I had a date with him last Monday.'

She shouldn't have told him that. It was the truth and it was innocent but she shouldn't have told him. He exploded. 'So it was *him* you went to the theatre with!'

'Yes. I didn't——'

'You said you'd gone with a friend,' he growled. 'And I assumed it was a friend of the female variety—which is what you supposed I would assume.'

'Demetrius, will you please listen to me?' Grace lowered her voice in the hope that it would calm him down. It didn't, his eyes were flashing dangerously and, whether it went against the grain or not, she knew that the wisest course would be another attempt to placate him. 'There's no need for this. Rodney is a friend and that's *all* he is! I can easily handle the likes of him.'

'Oh, really?' His eyes moved over her shoulder, narrowing as they found their target. 'He can't take his eyes off you, he's looking at you right now and I don't believe for one second that he regards you as nothing more than a friend! Make damned sure you keep away from him, do you hear me?'

She could do no more than stare at him, unable to believe what she'd heard. She didn't even attempt a retort, she walked away from him and headed upstairs to the bathroom. If she didn't take time to calm down, she would explode.

Keep away from him? From *Rodney*? For God's sake!

Like hell she would!

With a quick, unseeing look at herself in the mirror, she promptly went downstairs again. Demetrius was nowhere to be seen; maybe he had gone to cool off, too, he certainly needed it! She headed straight for the trio she had left only minutes earlier, and accepted instantly when Rodney asked her to dance. Let Demetrius make of this whatever he liked. If her relationship with him was to continue, he had to learn and learn now that he had gone too far this time.

She walked to the pool room with Rodney and moved stiffly into his arms, not realising her emotions were showing all over her face. She didn't stop to think that Demetrius was unaware of her defiance, that he wasn't here to see her dancing with the forbidden male. This was a matter of principle; why shouldn't she dance with an old friend?

'Good grief, lovely, loosen up a bit!' Rodney was laughing at her. 'And take that look off your face, anyone would think we were arch enemies!'

'I'm sorry.' She tried to relax, to smile at him. 'I'm a bit uptight. I—was surprised to see you here.'

He looked hurt, which in turn made her feel guilty. 'Did I do wrong in coming? Thomas said——'

'No, no, of course not. It's just——'

'It's just that you didn't invite me yourself.' He grinned at her. 'And why is that?'

'I wasn't short of an escort, that's why. I—imagined I'd have to stick by Thomas. You know parties aren't his thing.'

'Looks like little Melissa's entertaining him all right.' He moved in closer, holding her in a grip which was unnecessarily firm. Her breasts were pressing against his chest and she giggled, feeling her tension diminish slightly.

'Mr Featherstone, I believe you're drunk! I thought it the moment I saw you. Kindly ease up, will you? Have a little consideration for the dress!'

But Rodney wasn't laughing with her. His hand moved to the bare skin of her back and he lowered his head to brush a kiss against her cheek. 'God, Grace, you're such a turn-on!'

'Grace.' Suddenly there was another hand on her, its fingers biting in to her arm. Demetrius stepped between her and her dancing partner, his feelings barely contained. If she had thought him angry before, it was nothing compared to this! 'I want to talk to you. Now. You'll excuse us.'

He flung the last words at Rodney, steering Grace away from him, virtually marching her out of the room, oblivious to the curious looks they were getting. She was outraged, she felt like an errant child, but she was helpless to stop what he was doing. She thought her arm would snap in two as Demetrius steered her through the next room and into the hall. 'In here.' He opened the door of his office and pulled her roughly inside. He turned the key in the lock, removed it and dropped it in his jacket pocket.

'What the hell do you think you're doing?' she demanded. 'Open that door at once!'

He took hold of her with both hands this time, savagely, his grip causing her to gasp from the pain of it. In that same instant his mouth came down on hers with a punishing brutality she would never have thought him capable of. She fought for all she was worth, wrenching her head away. 'Dem——'

'I'm going to teach you a lesson, Grace, one you won't forget in a hurry. All that was for my benefit, was it not? That *display* out there! But a lot of other people had the benefit of it, too, or didn't you think of that? No, come to think of it you probably didn't—you conveniently forgot what you said to me the other night, and behaved as if I'm no more to you than your next-door neighbour!' His fury was almost tangible, and seeing him like this was another discovery—one she could have lived without. And he hadn't finished yet. 'What is it with you?' he went on. 'Are you ashamed to be associated with me?'

'Look, Demetrius——'

'Stop hedging! Either you are my woman or you're not.'

Defiantly she lifted her head. 'I am my own woman.'

He waved that away impatiently, his eyes raking hers. 'You know damn well what I mean. I just asked you a question.'

'All right, all right! No, of course I'm not ashamed of you. That's a crazy thing to say.'

'Is it? I'll bet my life you didn't tell Featherstone how it is with us. Well?'

'I——' He was right. She had let Rodney believe that Thomas was her escort tonight. 'No, I—I didn't.'

'Typical! What is it with you? Were you so scarred by the Raymond Ferris thing that you can't allow yourself to be seen enjoying another relationship? Not in front of family and friends, at any rate.'

Anger flared again. 'That is utterly ridiculous!'

'Oh, yes? I'll tell you what's ridiculous—you're terrified of any kind of commitment, even the mildest form of it.'

'That just isn't true! You and I—we're friends, aren't we?'

There was a sudden silence, a stillness that should have warned her of what was to come. Very quietly Demetrius said, 'Friends? All right, Grace, then let's see if you can handle me the way you tell me you can handle your other so-called friend.' Then his mouth was on hers again, and this time she couldn't pull her head away. He had pushed her against the wall, was pinning her there with his body.

Under the onslaught of his mouth, the entire length of him pressed against her, her body betrayed her in spite of the circumstances. Cursing herself, her own excitement, she vowed she would not let him see it. When he finally raised his head, slackened his hold, she brought her right arm up with the speed of light and slapped him hard across the cheek. 'How dare you treat me like that? I've taken more than enough from you tonight!'

He almost laughed at her, almost. It emerged as a short bark, and if she had hoped to shock him to his senses, she was sorely disillusioned. Her reaction had inflamed him, and he caught hold of both her hands, held them wide apart and flat against the wall. This time his body as well as his mouth ground against her, and within seconds she was made aware of his arousal.

The emotions raging inside her were unbelievably at odds. She was both angry and aroused at the same time. She was hating herself as well as him, was determined he wouldn't get the better of her... even though he was doing precisely that. When the quality of his kiss changed, when his lips suddenly gentled on hers, an involuntary moan was dragged from her, a small sound against his mouth.

Demetrius reacted to that with triumph, letting go of her abruptly so he could look down at her. 'I think I've proved my point,' he said quietly. The fingers of his left hand curled around the chain at her neck, and he gave a short tug, obliging her to move closer until her face was only inches from his. 'You're mine, Grace, mine for the taking. So don't ever again behave the way you did tonight. Do you understand me?'

Furiously, she slapped his hand away. It was too much. The triumphant look in his eyes, the dictatorial tones he used—it was far too much! 'Get away from me, Demetrius—get well away! When you put this chain around my neck, it did not make me your *slave*. No, I don't understand you. You're too possessive altogether, you like to think of me as yours—and you'd like everyone else to think in those terms—but the rules are different when it comes to your own behaviour.'

'What's that supposed to mean?'

'It means I am just as free as you are, that when you stay in London overnight, when you go partying——'

'*Partying?* Ah, I begin to understand! Melissa's behind this.' He smiled, but there was no humour in it. 'I don't know what she thought I was up to the last time I did that, but let me assure you I spent one of the most boring evenings of my life— at a dinner party at the home of my bank manager. Now, let's get something straight: there has been no one, no woman in my life since the day I met you. Don't look at me like that, I've never lied to you and I'm not about to start now. But you've lied to me, Grace, you've lied by omission.' His anger was back in full force now, fuelled by what he would say next. 'While I was sitting at home thinking about you last Monday, *you* were out with another man!'

'Demetrius, I don't see why you're making so much of this when I've explained to you several times——'

'Explained? Explained! Until tonight I'd never heard of Rodney Featherstone—then suddenly he's gate-crashing my party and slobbering all over my woman.'

'I am *not* your woman!'

His voice was soft then, dangerously so. 'Aren't you? You would still deny it?'

There was no contest, no escape. His hands were imprisoning her again—and this time there was a different kind of passion; it was not anger, but passion in the accepted sense of the word. He pulled her tightly against him, his hands on her ribs, his mouth shifting to her throat, to that place at the side of her neck . . .

Grace reached for him involuntarily, her body arching against his. She could see herself doing it, almost as if she were an observer. Still her mind was raging against what was happening—while her traitorous body revelled in it. When his hands moved to her breasts, she gasped loudly, shocked anew at the electrifying sensations he created in her. She had been wrong in thinking her attraction to Demetrius was strong; it was more than that, it was overwhelming. Never before had she experienced anything like it. Even through the covering of her dress he made her feel as if she was on fire, made her aware of every tingling nerve-end.

'Demetrius, please . . .' It had to stop, it had to stop now. She couldn't handle this, couldn't handle him. Couldn't handle herself. She was panicking. 'Stop this, please, *please*!'

He ignored her cries. Again, the mood of his kiss changed. He ran his tongue along the shell of her ear before claiming her mouth once more. Then his tongue was sliding over the inside of her lower lip, probing her mouth, pushing and withdrawing until she shuddered with the ecstasy, the sheer eroticism of it. Her arms were locked around him, under his jacket, and her fingers curled involuntarily, her nails digging into his back through the fine wool of his sweater.

It was just another source of encouragement to Demetrius. He shifted his stance, moving her the few inches which placed her against the wall again, his body forcing her legs apart as he got even closer to her, the strength of his arousal shocking her now. Quite suddenly she was afraid, more than she had ever been before. 'Demetrius, for God's sake... Let *go* of me! *Please!*'

She heard the catch in her voice and, to her relief, he did as she implored. He released her, but he stayed very, very close, looking down into her face. She could well imagine what she looked like, her hair tousled, her eyes unnaturally bright. Nervously, she ran her tongue over her lips, lips that were swollen and tingling.

He looked away from her when she did that, his voice unbelievably quiet as he spoke. 'Sit down, Grace.'

'I don't want to,' she whispered. 'I think——'

'I said sit down.'

She sat down. Against one wall of his office there was a leather settee and she lowered herself on to it, her entire body trembling, her heart leaping about wildly inside her breast. Her mind was tumbling in confusion, at odds with the dictates of her body and battling with the ambivalence of its own thoughts.

Not only had he tamed her into acquiescence, he had made it very clear that she *was* his for the taking. He had chosen to let her go, she had not fought him off. If he had carried on, he would have seduced her right here and now. She knew it. He knew it.

He knew it very well. He moved slowly across the room, leaned against his desk and looked at her steadily. He was no longer angry, but he was far from smiling. He spoke in a tone which was almost matter of fact. 'That's the score, Grace. I told you once before, you and I have unfinished business.'

The colour rose in her cheeks, but he ignored it. 'You asked me to give you time,' he went on, 'and I have to say I understand your reasons for that better now—once bitten, twice shy, and all that.'

'Demetrius——'

'Hear me out.' The edge was back in his voice. He looked at her evenly, going on slowly, as if warning her to listen and listen well. 'Quite apart from matters physical, I happen to like you, I like you very much. I think you feel the same way. I want to go on seeing you often and regularly, I want your company, and if you really don't wish to take things further than that, I'll respect your wish. How does it sound so far?'

'It sounds . . .' She was transfixed, her eyes were locked with his and, if her life had depended on it, she couldn't have looked away. She was almost mesmerised by him. She knew what he was going to say next, and she knew that what he had felt earlier was jealousy. Oh, it wasn't that his feelings for her went any deeper than liking, he was by nature a jealous man. Either she was or she was not going out with him, that was what he meant when he referred to her as his woman. She had a choice to make—Demetrius, and no one else, old friends included, or no Demetrius.

Melissa had once described him as passionate. He was, in every sense of the word. If he liked, he liked. And, no doubt, if he hated, he hated. There were no half-measures with Demetrius Knight, there was nothing half-hearted about him in any way at all. And in a way, although she admired this, it scared her.

But it didn't scare her enough. The thought of not seeing him again was abhorrent to her. 'It sounds good,' she said softly, still unable to break the hold of his eyes.

'Then you won't see Rodney Featherstone again.' It wasn't a question, it was a statement.

Grace shook her head. 'No. I mean, alone no. I can't really avoid——'

'Obviously I don't expect you to avoid him altogether, given the circumstances. I believe what you told me, that to you he's a friend and nothing more, but it's different for him—he fancies you, and please don't pretend you're not aware of it. Your insistence earlier that you can "handle" the likes of him was all I needed to hear. If he'd never made a pass at you there wouldn't be anything to handle, would there?'

'He's never done more than kiss me, Demetrius.' Even as she said this, she marvelled at herself. *Why* was she accounting to him like this? Because she had behaved badly, that was why. There was no denying it, and she had done it in front of his friends, in his own house. In retrospect, she could hardly blame him for his anger.

'And he's done that for the last time, Grace.'

'Yes,' she whispered. 'Yes.'

'That's all I wanted to hear. Now come here.'

And she did. His arms were open and she walked into them. He smiled, at last, and held her loosely. 'Do we understand each other now?'

She nodded, but it wasn't strictly true. If he knew how inexperienced she was in matters physical, he'd be staggered. In fact, he would never believe it, not after the way she'd responded to him. He had set out to prove a point tonight and he had done it

superlatively well. She was capable of being seduced. Well, admittedly she was. By him—but
never in a million years by Rodney. But how could
she tell Demetrius this? Explaining it would also
tell him of his specialness to her. No doubt such a
strong attraction was something he had experienced before, probably dozens of times, but it was
new to her.

She rested her head against his chest, deep in
thought. Dear lord, he was special, more so than
she had realised. He might not understand her fully,
but she understood him very well indeed. She knew
that he had told the truth, that when he spent the
night in London he would not be out with another
woman. He wouldn't demand of her something he
would be guilty of himself. He had too much integrity. He was a one-at-a-time man.

'Come on,' he said, his mouth against her temple,
'we'll get back to the party and we'll let *everyone*
see how it is with us.'

'Yes,' she said softly, aware that she was com-
mitting herself. But to what, exactly? How long was
she going to be able to keep her relationship with
him platonic? It was a worrying thought. And did
she want to? In a way, that was even more worrying... What kind of road had she just committed
herself to travelling with Demetrius? Where was it
going? He was obviously not the marrying kind.
Had he been, he wouldn't have got to thirty-six
without settling down.

CHAPTER EIGHT

From that night onward, Grace and Demetrius were seen to be a couple. As the days slipped into weeks, the entire county must have seen them together at one place or another, one event or another.

'It's getting pretty heavy with you two, isn't it?' Melissa remarked over lunch one day. She came regularly to The Beauty Parlour, enjoying having a facial, a manicure and, most importantly, a chat. Grace took her to lunch if she had the time, if she wasn't lunching with Demetrius. 'I don't know how you can fancy him, Grace. I couldn't fancy him if he were the last man on earth.'

'Of course you couldn't, he's your brother.'

'Speaking of brothers, how's yours?'

'He's fine, he phoned me last night. He sends you his regards.'

Melissa looked pleased, Thomas always sent his regards. 'He's sweet. In a way, he reminds me of——'

She didn't finish the sentence, but Grace knew what she'd been about to say; she was thinking of the boy in Athens, surely. She waited, giving Melissa the opportunity to talk about it if she wanted to. She didn't.

'Not quite a word I'd choose.' Grace laughed, but she in turn was thinking...about Melissa's opening remark.

Heavy, pretty heavy. Was it, in fact? She was still calling a halt with Demetrius, when she was in his

arms and there was a danger of things going too
far. She still wasn't ready or willing to take the
plunge in that respect. If she did, surely it would
be the beginning of the end? It would be an affair,
an unforgettable, wildly passionate affair, for sure,
but in time it would burn itself out and it would
end...would end. When it ended. It was not a
pleasant prospect. It was, however, an inevitable
one.

Demetrius had led a very different life from hers,
he had told her about some of his affairs. By his
own admission, there had been plenty of them. Admission? He had simply told her the facts. She had
asked him, very casually, whether he had ever
thought of marrying. His reply had been quick and
wry. 'No danger.'

Clearly, that was still his attitude towards marriage. And why should a man in his position seek
a permanent relationship? As she had thought
about him before, he had everything going for him.
Not that she was thinking of herself as a candidate;
far from it, she, too, had a full and satisfactory life
as it was.

She was happy with the status quo, she liked to
think she was calling the shots in keeping things
platonic with Demetrius—well, keeping out of his
bed, at least. Platonic was hardly the word. Yet she
knew very well that he was merely allowing her to
do this; he had proved to her once that if he made
up his mind to have her, she would be helpless to
resist.

But he hadn't done that, which begged another
question. Why hadn't he? Sometimes, perversely,
Grace came close to feeling indignant when he accepted her calling a halt to their lovemaking. She

could only assume she wasn't as irresistible to him as she liked to think. On the other hand she was grateful to him for letting her have control. It was all a bit confusing really, the way he was being so patient with her when he was not a patient man.

All in all, she was happy, but at the same time she felt insecure. She knew she was in danger of falling in love with him. If she did...what then?

She looked at him carefully that evening, when they were settled in the drawing-room after one of Matty's delicious dinners. Demetrius was sprawled on a settee and Grace was in her father's armchair near the fireplace, gauging his mood. 'Demetrius...'

'Yes, my darling?'

She returned his smile. He had taken to calling her that of late, always with the possessive pronoun, of course. 'I had lunch with Melissa today and—I want to talk to you about her.'

'Yes?'

'Does she ever mention—no, of course she wouldn't. Not to you.'

'Not to me—what?'

'The boy in Greece.'

He seemed surprised but not annoyed. 'She's told you about that? What has she told you?'

'Very little. I don't know any details, but—well, I have the feeling she's still pining for him.'

'I shouldn't be surprised.'

Grace looked at him quickly. It had not been a sympathetic retort. 'Is that all you have to say?'

'I'm sorry, I can't comment any further. Unless and until Melissa tells you about this herself, it would be out of order for me to discuss it with you.'

She couldn't help but admire him for that; she respected it. As close as they were, he felt he

shouldn't tell her something which was obviously
very personal about his sister. He was, she thought,
quite a character, a strong character who wrote his
own code of conduct and stuck to it.

'That's fair enough.' She yawned, stretching her
legs out in front of her. 'It's getting late, Demetrius,
it's time to throw you out if we're going riding in
the morning.'

He made no move. 'And if I say we won't, that
you can have an extra hour in bed, what then?'

She raised an eyebrow. 'If you suppose for one
minute that I don't notice the way you manipulate
me, you'd better think again. You just love getting
your own way all the time, don't you?'

'Who doesn't?' He patted the settee, his smile
was back and it was bordering on the lecherous.
'Come over here and smother me with kisses.'

She laughed her head off at that. 'Mm, maybe
I will—but only because I'd do anything for an
extra hour in bed!' She was already moving towards
him, her laughter fading as he reached for her. It
was she who kissed him, little kisses, dozens of
them. A bargain was a bargain, after all.

Then he caught her to him more tightly, stilling
the movement of her mouth by covering it with his
own. It was a long time before he lifted his head,
his fingers reaching to smooth the silky hair from
her forehead. He was intensely serious when he
spoke. 'There's a lot that I would do for an hour
in bed. With you. A great deal, my darling. I
wonder if you know how much?'

The hammering of her heart accelerated. It was
always like that when she was in his arms, and the
look in his eyes now was almost stopping her
breathing. She didn't know what to say. Even if she

had been inspired, she doubted she could speak. To make matters worse, her face was colouring. Why was it he could make that happen to her so easily?

'So nothing changes,' he said quietly, letting go of her. 'How long do you expect to keep this up, Grace? When are you going to come to me, willingly? When will your mind catch up with the dictates of your body?' He reached for her again, just with one hand, letting it move ever so lightly across her breasts, making her blush more deeply, because he was so damned accurate in what he'd said.

Grace didn't move, she couldn't, she still couldn't find her voice, either. And it got worse. In the same quiet tone, one which almost bordered on sadness, he said, 'Why the blush? If you have inhibitions of some sort I can only say I'm surprised, and I don't understand them. I certainly don't share them.' He took hold of her hand and guided it towards his body, making her aware how very much he wanted her, as if she didn't already know. She was swamped with guilt. How much more of this would he tolerate?

'You're keeping me awake at night, you must realise that. It can't go on for ever. I think it's time you made a decision, don't you?'

He got to his feet and Grace looked up at him rapidly. She was panic-stricken. 'Are you—is that an ultimatum?'

'An ultimatum?' He didn't seem to know what she meant.

She didn't move. She could think more clearly when she wasn't touching him or being touched by him. She was still panicking, but she also experienced a ripple of annoyance. 'Don't give me an ultimatum, Demetrius, because that would be the quickest way of hearing me say goodbye.'

'*What?* Would you mind telling me what you're rambling about, woman?'

She didn't know whether he was angry or amused. 'I thought—I mean . . .'

'You thought I was demanding more than you want to give, that's what you mean.' His tone was patient, fortunately. 'And if you weren't forthcoming, that it would be I who would say goodbye.' He shook his head, as if disappointed in her. 'I thought you knew me better than that. Don't you know by now how stubborn I am? I want you and I shall have you, sooner or later. It's as simple as that.'

She was half smiling, half indignant. 'Is it, by God?'

He reached down and grabbed her wrist, wrenching her to her feet—but he was laughing now. 'Yes, by God. So if you want to make a bet on it, you'll lose.'

'No bets,' she said softly, wanting desperately to move into his arms but thinking better of it. As it was, she could feel the heat of his body, only inches away from hers. 'Say goodnight, Demetrius.'

'Goodnight, Demetrius,' he said, and left.

Grace upset her father towards the end of May. She didn't mean to, but it was when he phoned during mid-week to tell her he wasn't coming home for the weekend . . . the third weekend in a row.

'No, I won't be lonely.' She smiled at his question. Lonely? With Demetrius? Hardly. 'But I miss seeing you,' she added honestly. 'If you stay away this weekend, it'll be a month since I saw you last. Hang on, I've just thought of something. Demetrius and I are going to the ballet on Saturday. Why don't we come into London during the afternoon and have an early dinner with you? You'll be in your house, won't you?'

She expected him to say yes, and naturally she expected Phyllis would be there. But Sir Nigel was going away for the weekend. 'To meet Phyllis' son—well, to meet his wife, actually. I have met her son once, briefly. He and his family live in Warwickshire and after my surgery on Saturday morning we're driving up there, spending the weekend.'

His surgery... he meant the period in which he was available to his constituents. 'I see. Is Phyllis there with you now?'

'Yes, she's in the kitchen.' There was a smile in his voice. 'Do you want a word with her?'

'No, don't disturb her. I was wondering—er— how is it going with you two?'

There was a burst of enthusiasm. 'It's going beautifully, beautifully. You wouldn't believe how much we have in common.'

Grace did know the feeling, it was like that with her and Demetrius. It was then that she dropped her clanger. 'Has she actually moved in with you?'

'Grace! You can't be serious!'

'Why not?' She had been serious, and so what? She was soon put straight.

'You young people might have discarded all standards of proper behaviour, but we old fogies still give a damn. Most of us, at any rate. There are plenty of people who still believe in marriage, young lady, and I sincerely hope that you're one of them. Phyllis and I certainly do. She is not the sort of woman who would live with a man, and I am not the sort of man who would expect that, or desire it. Quite apart from all that, I have a reputation to maintain, or have you forgotten? And so has Phyllis. How you could even ask ... Are you still there, Grace?'

'I'm here, Daddy. I'm sorry I spoke.' She was grinning, trying not to let it show in her voice. Perhaps it had been a silly question. 'So you're going to marry her, are you?'

Silence.

'Daddy?'

'I'm thinking about it.'

'Thinking about your answer, or thinking about marrying her?'

'I don't know what's got in to you, miss. I have *not* popped the question, but I *am* thinking of doing so. Soon, actually. Does that satisfy you?'

'Perfectly.'

'So you'll just have to wait and see.' There was a pause. Grace thought that was the end of their conversation but it wasn't. It was her turn to be grilled. 'And what about you and Demetrius?'

She felt herself stiffen. 'What about us?' Was her father teaching her a lesson, telling her she shouldn't have asked the questions she had asked? Or did he really want to know?

'I hope you're not about to tell me to mind my own business, Grace?'

'No,' she said cautiously. 'Is that what you're trying to tell me?'

'No, darling, it isn't. I want you to know my plans. It was just your suggestion that we might be living—what is the expression?—over the brush, which offended.'

'I'm sorry about that.' Grace was stalling for time. 'Um—everything's fine with me and Demetrius.'

'Then maybe he's thinking of popping the question?'

Another silence.

She didn't know how she was going to tell him that, with Demetrius, popping the question was out of the question. 'I—can't imagine him as the marrying kind, Daddy. He—he seems very happy as a bachelor. I think he believes it to be the perfect state.'

'Rubbish. Firstly, he can't compare the two states, he's only known the one, secondly, I simply don't believe that. From what I can gather, he's seeing you seven nights a week. To what end, one asks oneself?'

'It isn't seven nights a week. It's . . . five or six,' she added lamely.

'And you're splitting hairs.'

'Look, Demetrius and I are . . . just friends.'

'What you mean is, you'll be content just having an affair with him.'

'I am not having an affair with him!'

Sir Nigel sighed. 'That wasn't an accusation, Grace. I'm not *that* stuffy, you know, not so old-fashioned, or perhaps I should say unrealistic, that I expect my twenty-four-year-old daughter to be a virgin.'

She groaned inwardly, wishing this conversation was not happening. Oh, how little he knew! It was ironic. It seemed he assumed she was either having an affair with Demetrius and not admitting it, or that she had gone to bed with Raymond Ferris five years earlier. In a voice which was a touch more

aggressive than she meant it to be, she said, 'As
you often say to journalists, no comment.' Then,
with more aggression, 'Just answer me this. Are
you telling me it would be all right to have an affair
with Demetrius, but it wouldn't be all right to live
with him?'

Sir Nigel was shocked again. 'Is that what you're
thinking of doing?'

'No.' As if Demetrius would want that! She was
handy as it was, being next door. 'No way. I'm just
interested to know what you would sanction and
what you wouldn't—though I shall please myself
anyway, as you know. I'm not nineteen any more.'

Another silence. Grace broke it; she had made
an unnecessary remark and she regretted it. 'I'm
sorry, that was below the belt.'

'Yes, it was. And all I can say to it is that
Demetrius Knight is very, very different from
Raymond Ferris. I should be delighted if Demetrius
were to become my son-in-law.'

'Well, he won't. So answer my question.'

'I'll give you my opinion, certainly. If two people
want to live together and are thinking in terms of
permanence, why not marry? If they're serious, if
it's going to be for keeps, why not marry? There
are so many advantages, social, practical as well as
psychological.'

'Psychological?'

'Marriage represents commitment, a commitment made in public, being sure enough and proud
enough to state your intentions in public. Showing
one's partner that one is serious.'

Grace looked heavenward. 'Don't get me wrong,
I'm not arguing against marriage, definitely not.
But I would point out that the little piece of paper

called a marriage certificate can make for plenty of
problems if one wishes to call it a day.'

'Precisely!' Sir Nigel was triumphant. 'So people
opt for living together—because they're *not*
thinking in terms of forever, not sure enough to get
tied up with that piece of paper. See what I mean?'

Grace couldn't help laughing at him. 'Did you
ever think of going in to politics, Father dear? You
argue well. If you were here with me now, however,
I would keep you at this discussion for at least two
hours . . . and I'd probably pull your argument to
pieces. Just as an intellectual exercise, of course,
not necessarily with my own beliefs. But I have to
go now. Demetrius is taking me out and he's due
here in twenty minutes.'

Sir Nigel wasn't laughing. 'Grace? May I end with
a bit of fatherly advice?'

'Of course,' she said warmly, loving him. He was
a good man and he was entitled to his opinions.
'Go on.'

'Just—be careful not to get pregnant. That could
really complicate matters.'

She had already thought of that. A hundred
times. She had thought of getting herself the Pill,
but . . . she hadn't got round to it. She said goodbye
to her father and went to get ready for Demetrius.
The conversation had depressed her.

There was, she knew, a storm brewing. Last
Saturday, Demetrius had lost patience with her for
the first time. They had been here in the manor
because they knew they could be alone except for
Matty, who didn't count. Matty had been in bed
for hours, Grace and Demetrius had been talking
for hours when, inevitably, they had ended up
together on the settee. It had been difficult then.

She had actually fought him off the moment his hands had moved to her breasts. She had had to, for she had wanted him before he'd even touched her, had been looking at him from a distance of some yards and had been aroused purely by their conversation, an intense discussion which had stimulated more than her brain. It had got to the stage where just listening to him was a turn-on, he had been so intense about what he was saying, had looked so damned attractive.

'Grace...' She hadn't anticipated what he was going to say when she had pushed his hands away. It hadn't been a pleasant scene. 'For God's sake, what's the matter? I've never known anyone like you, not since I was sixteen, anyhow!'

'I'm sorry——'

'You're not sorry. Like hell you're sorry. You're deliberately winding me up and——'

'No!' She had been horrified. 'No, I'm not doing that. On the contrary, I'm trying to prevent it!'

He had looked at her as if she was crazy. 'Then I suggest you keep your distance.'

'I—perhaps you'd better go home now.'

'Too right!' He had left then. Grace had stayed where she was, thinking. And getting nowhere. Some time ago he had suggested she make a decision. She still hadn't. And time was running out now.

He had been fine when she saw him the following day, but...there was a storm brewing, she was sure of it.

She was right. It happened on the following Sunday. They weren't alone in the house, but it made no difference. They were in Demetrius' house. The three of them had had a swim, Melissa had cooked dinner and went to bed around ten o'clock, leaving her brother and Grace alone in the sitting-room. They were curled up on the settee, a four-seater affair as wide as a single bed and just as soft. They were watching a play on TV when Melissa left them. At least, they were for half an hour or so.

Then they were in one another's arms and Demetrius was kissing her hungrily. When his hands slid to her thighs, beneath the folds of her skirt, Grace didn't worry about it. Nor did she when he pushed the straps of her blouse aside, pulling it down. She was bra-less, she almost always was, and for a moment Demetrius just gazed at her, looking at her as if she were some kind of goddess. 'Grace! You are so incredibly beautiful...'

She was too pleased to laugh. She wasn't beautiful, her body was good but she didn't think of herself as beautiful. Demetrius was of a different opinion; he was looking at her in wonder, his eyes glittering, black, hungry... His hands were still on her thighs and slid to her hips, pulling her towards him, positioning her body so she was lying down, shifting himself so he was on top of her, taking his weight on one elbow. It all happened so quickly, so easily, the way he took control, the way he covered the tip of her breast with his mouth.

It was the first time he had done that, and it shocked her into a response—a response he didn't want. She tried to push him away. 'Demetrius——'

He lost his temper, swiftly, completely and violently. He wrenched away from her, was on his feet in a flash, looking down at her and accusing her, demanding answers. 'I don't believe it, I just don't believe this! What the *hell* is the matter with

you? What do you think I'm made of, what are
you trying to do to me? What do you *want* of me,
for God's sake?'

She had covered herself up before his first
question was out, as fast as she could. Tears had
sprung to her eyes and there was no possibility of
stopping them, there were too many emotions
churning inside her, burning inside her. The tears
welled up and trickled from her eyes. It made things
worse.

'Don't *do* that!' Demetrius yelled. He turned his
back on her, every muscle of his body rigid, the
fingers of one hand raking through his hair in frustration. 'I can't take it, Grace. I've had enough.
What the hell do you want from me?'

'Nothing.' It was hardly more than a whisper.
She was scared, her insides knotted with tension.
She was already on her feet and was groping for
her bag at the side of the settee, knowing she had
to get out of there. The trouble was that she
couldn't see very well. She swiped at her eyes with
the back of her hand.

'Answer me!' he bellowed. 'What the devil is
going on here?'

Enough, it was enough. She couldn't stand this,
the sheer volume of his voice was enough to make
her tremble. There was no consolation in seeing that
his hands were trembling, too. She spun around and
glared at him. 'Nothing! Leave me alone. I'm
looking—where did you put my handbag? Find it,
so I can get out of here!'

'You're not going anywhere.' In a single stride,
he crossed over to where she was standing, his hands
clamping on the bare skin of her shoulders, shaking
her. 'Answer me. I want some answers!'

Grace's mind had gone blank. She couldn't remember any specific question, she couldn't think at all, he was shaking the sense out of her. 'I don't— I can't...' She started crying in earnest, great, gasping sobs.

Suddenly the world was still again, the room was still, her head was cradled against his chest, his hand stroking her hair as he apologised over and over. 'Grace, Grace my darling, forgive me. I'm sorry, I'm so sorry. Don't cry. Please stop that. I—I just...' He broke off, sighing, still holding her head against his chest. 'I just don't know what I'm going to do about you. You're driving me out of my mind.' Softly, irresistibly so, he added, 'Please, Grace, *please* tell me why you're so hung-up.'

She pulled away, staring up at him. He was speaking from the heart, and she had to give him an answer, a straight answer. She owed it to him. 'I'm not hung-up, Demetrius. I'm just not the— the...' She couldn't go on, she didn't know how to say it.

'What?' His eyes were pleading with her. 'What? Say it, Grace. Have you had a bad sexual experience with someone, is that it?'

Oh, God! She looked away, then she turned away and kept her back to him. It was no use, she had to tell him. 'No. The problem is ... well, half the problem is ... I haven't had any experience at all.'

She honestly thought she would die, the silence screamed at her so. It was awful, endless, saying so very much. It went on, it went on for so long that she started walking towards the door without looking back.

'*Grace, wait.*'

She stopped dead, going rigid. She had been unable to interpret what was behind his voice. She did not turn around, not until he told her to.

'Look at me.' It came quietly, gently. 'Turn around, you idiot, and look at me.'

She turned. Her face was pink, but she didn't even know it this time.

'So what happens next?' he said, his eyes on hers.

'I—don't know.'

'Then let me make a suggestion. Marry me.'

'*What?*' She thought she shouted the word; in fact, it hardly got past her lips. But Demetrius caught it.

'I said, marry me. That's what you want, isn't it, Grace?'

Stunned, she was so utterly stunned, so appalled, that she couldn't speak for a moment. '*Marry* you! Why?' she demanded. 'So you can get your hands on my body? Legally? Legitimately? Is that how your mind is working? You must think me pathetic, pathetic!'

He gaped at her. 'Pathetic? What the hell do you mean——'

'Well, maybe I am!' She was shouting now. It wasn't just her hands that were trembling, her entire body was trembling. 'I've obviously given you more—pain—than I realised. I apologise for that. If you wanted to hurt me in return, you've succeeded. I might lack experience, Demetrius, but I do not lack intelligence. Do you think I'd marry someone, anyone, for such a stupid reason? Do you think I'm so "hung-up" that I have to marry before I can give myself to a man?' Her voice rose, almost hysterically. 'Why should I want to do that? Why should I—why should I do *anything* I don't want

to do? Going to bed with you included. Stuff your
stupid suggestion, stuff it back down your throat
where it came from. Marriage is *not* what I want,
to you or anyone else. You insult me, I realise full
well what you're accusing me of. You think I've
been angling for this, don't you? Holding you off
like some Victorian maiden, in the hope that it
would do the trick and get you to propose.'

'Grace——'

She jumped on him, hard and fast. He wasn't
going to get away with this. She was right and she
knew it. 'Shut up! Don't insult me any further. I'm
sick of being made to feel guilty, I'm sick of being
pressurised, of your so-called patience with me. I'm
nothing more than a challenge to you, I see that
now. It's down to the old male ego thing, isn't it?
Or your Greek blood or something. You're determined to have me no matter at what price!' Her
handbag was almost under her nose, she spotted it
on the sideboard and grabbed it.

'Goddammit, Grace, will you listen to me?'

'No!' She almost screamed at him. 'No, I've
heard enough, I'm going.' She was already flinging
the door open. 'Stay away from me. Find yourself
another woman, one who won't try to manipulate
and manoeuvre you into making a proposal of
marriage. Ha! *Marriage!* The word wasn't even in
your vocabulary an hour ago. My God, you really
are frustrated, aren't you?'

There was just time to see the expression on his
face before she bolted. If he had been angry with
her before, she couldn't think what word would describe how he felt in that moment. Nor did she stick
around to find out. Even if she'd wanted to stay
around, she wouldn't have dared.

Fortunately, he didn't pursue her. Unfortunately, she didn't have her car with her. The nights were getting lighter with every passing day and she had walked to his house. It was chilly now, not that she registered the fact. Tears were pouring down her face and she was experiencing a frustration which was totally alien to her. It was physical, mental, emotional—everything combined.

Hurrying home, blindly, stumbling from time to time, she felt in those moments that she hated Demetrius. And she hated herself. Why hadn't she simply behaved like the normal, red-blooded girl she actually was? Life would be so much simpler. Why did she have to complicate things?

It wasn't until she got into bed that she began to calm down. She heard the telephone ringing and she ignored it, knowing it would be him, dreading it would be him.

Hoping it was him.

It kept ringing, and ringing. She put her head under her pillow and started crying again. Still the phone rang, and rang. She wanted to scream, she wanted to pick it up. She did neither, she just cried, quietly now, resignedly.

It was another hour before everything became clear to her, before her tears abated and she became thoroughly calm, almost unnaturally calm. Suddenly she knew the answer to all her questions, and to most of his. Suddenly, shockingly, she knew why she had become so uncharacteristically violent with him. She knew why she was reluctant to make love with him. She knew why his suggestion of marriage had insulted her to such an extent. It was not what he wanted, it was just the price he was prepared to pay, *her* price, as he thought. But for her . . . for her, marriage to Demetrius was a glorious and glittering prospect.

In other words, she was in love with him. It explained it all. She loved him, very, very deeply.

She turned over in bed, in the hope that she would go to sleep. At least she knew, now, what it was that ailed her. But as Demetrius had said, 'So what happens next?'

That was one question she did not have the answer to.

CHAPTER NINE

JILLIAN was just making coffee when the phone rang in The Beauty Parlour the next morning. Grace reached for it. She hadn't slept at all the previous night, not even for an hour, and her nerves were jangling. She didn't want to be in work, but they were fully booked that morning. Melissa was among the bookings and was due in at eleven-thirty.

She took a deep breath, certain it would be Demetrius ringing. 'The Beauty Parlour, may I help you?'

'Grace? At last! I was ringing you for ages last night. It was late, but I know you're rarely in bed before midnight.'

It was her father, his voice animated, excited. She felt sick; she had been so sure it was Demetrius calling. Last night and now. But it wasn't, hadn't been. 'No, Daddy. I—was probably in the bath or something.'

'Are you all right?' Her despondency was obviously showing in her voice, and she made a monumental effort to brighten up. He had something important to tell her. Why else would he ring her so late at night, so early in the morning?

Grace didn't need three guesses as to his news. She psyched herself up to give the right response, determined not to let him down with lack of enthusiasm. 'I'm fine, Daddy, absolutely fine. What about you? Did you have a good weekend?'

155

'Phyllis and I didn't get back to London till eleven or so last night. We had a good weekend in Warwickshire, very successful. Did I mention that her daughter was taking the train up from Cambridge? Oh. Well, she did. So we were all together, her daughter, her son and his family. He has two delightful boys, aged three and four.'

Grace waited while he rambled, smiling to herself in spite of her depression. How proper her father was! He had had to meet all Phyllis' family, get their nod of approval, had brought Phyllis to meet his family, had had their nod of approval. And then... 'Anyway, we got back around eleven, as I say. I dropped her off and—and guess what?'

'What?' She wasn't going to steal his thunder.

'I asked her to marry me and she accepted!'

'Oh, Daddy, that's marvellous!'

'Isn't it just?'

'Have you set the date?'

'Not the actual date, but we'll marry in August, probably the latter half.'

'August? But that's ages away, why wait so long?'

'Parliament, of course. We intend to have a three- or four-week honeymoon, so we're waiting until they recess for the summer holidays.'

Parliament. Of course. 'Well, that *is* good news. Congratulations, Daddy!'

'Thank you, darling. I'll talk to you later. 'Bye.'

He hung up, leaving her to stare at the telephone. It had been no surprise, but—well, she just hoped she had reacted appropriately. She was happy for him. For Phyllis, too.

'Your coffee, Grace.' Jillian put a steaming cup in front of her, smiling. 'If you'll forgive me for saying so, you look as if you need this. You OK?'

'I'm fine.'

'I wouldn't go that far. Did you have a rotten weekend?'

Grace looked up at her, nodding. 'Rotten.'

Belle Wakeham came in then; she tied her pet poodle to the leg of the cane sofa in the reception area, beaming broadly. 'What a beautiful day, Grace!'

Was it? She hadn't noticed. It crossed her mind that she could tell Belle her father's news, but she didn't. He would probably want to tell people himself, which was understandable. Even when Belle mentioned Sir Nigel, Grace kept quiet about his forthcoming marriage.

'How's your father, Grace?'

'He's fine, thanks.'

'And Phyllis?'

Grace nodded. When she had told her of Phyllis Radcliffe's visit to the manor over Easter, Belle had admitted that she knew Phyllis. 'I knew your father was seeing her in London, but I couldn't say anything to you because Phyllis told me you didn't know—when they first started seeing one another, I mean.'

'They were silly, don't you think?' Grace had laughed at the time. 'Daddy seemed to think I might have some objection. He kept it such a big secret, or so he thought—as if it's any of my business.'

'Well, I've known Phyllis for years. She was a patient of my husband over twenty years ago, when we lived in London. I see her from time to time, when I go in to town. We have lunch together occasionally. As a matter of fact, your mother met her once, only once to my knowledge. It was years ago, I introduced your mother to her, the three of us had lunch and they got on well. It's rather a nice thought that, isn't it?'

Grace had agreed. A nice thought, that her mother had liked the woman her husband would marry many years later.

'Life is strange, isn't it?' Belle said now. 'I think your father will end up marrying Phyllis, don't you?'

'I shouldn't be surprised.' Grace glanced at her watch, a gesture that was misunderstood.

'Am I holding you up, dear?'

'No, no. I just—I'd lost track of the time, that's all.' It was almost nine. Demetrius would have been in his office for an hour by now. Would he ring her?

Should she ring him?

'I'll get on, anyway,' Belle said. She was having half an hour on the sun-bed to begin with, as usual. Grace let her go, glancing uncertainly at the telephone. She was getting a headache, there was a tight band of pressure from temple to temple, and the tension inside her was chronic.

What if he didn't ring her? What if it was...*over*? She was still angry about his proposal, it had been a crazy thing to say. But it had been said on the spur of the moment, when he was hardly himself. Was she making excuses for him? Yes. Still, the idea of not seeing him again was intolerable, intolerable. That and so many other thoughts were combining to make her feel dizzy.

She went into the tiny kitchen in search of some aspirin. Jillian was there, having a quick cigarette and a cup of coffee before she started work. Grace took the aspirin and locked herself in the loo. It

was the only place she was assured of privacy. She
had to think.

Ten minutes later she emerged. She had made a
decision, she was going to ring Demetrius. Mavis
was already with her first client, and Jillian's first
client was in reception, was just being shown to a
cubicle by her. The coast was clear.

She picked up the receiver and dialled, asking for
extension nineteen when she got through.

'I'm sorry,' she was told, 'Mr Knight's extension
is engaged. He's been on the telephone all morning,
actually.' Grace was privy to this information,
probably because her voice was so familiar to the
switchboard. They knew her by now at the offices
of DKK Holdings. 'Can I take a message, have him
ring you back?'

She lost her nerve. 'No, I—you needn't mention
I called.' The instant she hung up, the phone jangled
and she picked it up again.

'Grace? You were engaged a moment ago. Listen,
something's come up.' It was Demetrius, sounding
as if nothing at all had happened between them!
She couldn't say a word, her heart was thumping
so hard she could barely breathe.

'It's a damned nuisance, but I have to go to
Scotland for a few days,' he went on. 'I'm not sure
when I'll be back, but we can certainly fix a date
for the end of the week. Friday night at the latest,
I'll definitely be back by then.' There was a pause.
'Are you there, Grace?'

'I'm here. I—just tried to ring you, actually.'

'You did?' His pleasure, his relief, was unconcealed. Quietly he added, 'I thought...I didn't think
you would ring me.'

'I didn't think you'd ring me.' There were tears in her eyes. She closed them. Dear God, she loved him so much! She couldn't fight it any longer, not any longer. 'I'll look forward to seeing you on Friday at the latest, then.'

'If I'm going to be home sooner I'll ring you. Please keep an eye on Melissa while I'm away.' Another pause. 'I want to talk to you, Grace. I'm only sorry I can't see you tonight.'

So was she, not that there was anything to talk about, in her opinion. What was there to say, really? Hadn't they said it all, thrashed it all out, last night? She didn't see that talking was going to get them anywhere, something far more positive was needed.

'We'll have dinner on Friday,' Demetrius was saying. 'We'll go out so we can be sure of being alone.'

'No.' Grace said the word firmly, as firmly as her mind was made up. 'Come to my house. I doubt very much whether my father will come home this weekend. So we'll have dinner there, alone, and when Matty's gone to bed, we'll go to bed.'

The silence that followed seemed endless.

When Demetrius spoke, it was in a voice so neutral, she couldn't begin to guess what he was thinking. 'Would you care to repeat what you just said? I don't think I caught it.'

She repeated it.

Then she knew what he was thinking, at least, she knew he was furious with her. 'If I could spare the time, I'd come round there, put you over my knee and wallop you! Do you hear me? Unfortunately, I can't because I have to leave right now. So I'll pretend I didn't hear what you said. I'll be in touch.'

He hung up before she could say another word. Again she was staring at the phone, but this time she was at a loss to believe what she'd heard. Never in a million years would she have expected him to react like that! What was he so angry about? What had she done wrong now? Surely he ought to have been—*what* was the matter with the man?

It was a busy, fraught Monday morning. The phone kept ringing, or so it seemed, two people came in on chance, without appointments, and had to be turned away, and when Melissa arrived at eleven-thirty she was in a state of excitement so acute that Grace didn't know what to do with her.

'I have to talk to you!' The words came bubbling from the younger girl before the bell on the outer door had stopped tinkling. 'Can we skip the facial and go out for a cup of coffee, instead?'

'A cup of coffee?' Grace repeated the words blankly. Melissa's cheeks were flushed with excitement, her dark eyes glowing. 'But—what's up?'

'Nothing, everything. Oh, it's all so marvellous, Grace! But you've got to help me, you've just *got* to. If you don't, I . . . I don't know what I'll do!' Her face clouded, changing from radiance to near despair in a split second.

Grace didn't even try to make sense of it, she gave in and agreed to go out for coffee. Melissa had booked an hour of her time, so it made no difference to anyone or anything. 'Give me a moment. I'll just have a word with Jillian and switch the telephone answering-machine on. Do sit down a moment, Melissa, stop hopping around like that, you're making me nervous.'

Getting more agitated than she was already was to be avoided. Ever since Demetrius' phone call,

Grace had been on pins. She was dreading Friday rather than looking forward to it, couldn't imagine what he wanted to say to her...let alone what he had made of her offer to go to bed with him. She had thought she understood the man very well, but she was beginning to doubt that now.

'You know Demetrius has had to go to Scotland?' The question came from Melissa, who couldn't bring herself to sit down. 'He phoned me just before my taxi came.'

'Yes, he phoned me, too.'

'You two had a fight last night, didn't you? I heard your raised voices, but I couldn't make out what you were saying.'

Grace looked at her quickly. Had she really not made out what had been said? 'That's none of your business.'

'I know it isn't. I'm not asking.' There was a careless shrug. Grace marvelled at it. Whatever was eating at the girl had to be very important indeed.

Fifteen minutes later, Grace got to hear about it. They had gone to a coffee shop next door but one. Melissa didn't even touch her cup. 'I've found the course I want to do! It's perfect!'

'The course?' For a moment Grace didn't know what she was referring to. 'What course?'

'Grace! The course in interior design and decoration, what do you think I'm talking about?'

'But...but you haven't said anything really positive about this in weeks——'

'I couldn't until I'd decided exactly what I was going to do, where I was going, could I? I had to plan properly, it's what Demetrius would expect. I've been writing off all over the place, and I've had millions of prospectuses. Well, dozens. The course I've found is perfect, perfect! It's a two-year, full-time course and it's very comprehensive. They teach not only—oh, but never mind the curriculum. More importantly, it's a private course, so that will involve fees—but that's all right, Demetrius won't mind paying for me.'

Grace waited. What Melissa had just said was true...so why was she suddenly looking glum? 'Go on,' she said ominously. 'I've had the good news, let's hear the bad news.'

Melissa raised her head, she was very near to tears. 'Oh, Grace, you've got to help me. If you don't, Demetrius will never buy the idea.'

'Get to the point, Melissa. Explain yourself.'

'Well, it's...the course is at an academy in Paris.'

'Paris?'

'You see! If that's your reaction, you can imagine how Demetrius will feel about it.'

'But why Paris? Surely you could find something suitable in England, in London? Why Paris, for heaven's sake?'

'Because it's what I want, that's why. I have a friend there, an ex-schoolfriend who lives there with her parents. I've kept in touch with her since we left the convent. Her parents are very respectable, they have a huge house and...I can live with them.'

It was beginning to make sense, a little. 'Have they said so?'

'I got a letter this morning. They said they'll be delighted, it will be company for Marianne. She's an only child, you see. She's at college, too.'

'Have you actually been accepted on the course? What about having an interview? I thought——'

'There wasn't any need. I wrote and told them all they needed to know about me. I speak French as well as I speak Greek and English, you know.'

'No, I hadn't realised that. Go on.'

'There isn't much more to tell. I left school with more than enough qualifications.'

So she had, Demetrius had told her that.

'In any case,' Melissa went on, 'I've told you, it's a private thing, fee-paying. Why should they refuse me?'

'Why indeed? Well, haven't you been the busy little bee? Er—I take it you haven't mentioned this to Demetrius yet?'

Melissa's shoulders slumped. 'What do you think? I heard from the academy two weeks ago, and I wrote again to my friend to tell her I'd been accepted. The letter inviting me to live with them came from her parents after Demetrius had left the house this morning. When he phoned me earlier I had no chance to say anything except *bon voyage*. He was whizzing off to London, picking up some clothes from his apartment before he took the shuttle to Edinburgh. Business calls and all that. He just told me to behave myself—and he warned me that you would be keeping an eye on me. How's that for trust?'

Grace smiled. 'But what's the problem? Why do you need my help? What sort of help?'

'You just don't understand, do you? My *passport*. Demetrius has it under lock and key, remember? I want to go to Paris earlier than I need to, there's nothing to keep me here. I want to get to know the place, spend some time with Marianne during the summer holidays. But I—I don't think Demetrius will let me go at all.'

'He still thinks there's a danger of your taking off for Greece, is that it?'

Melissa nodded miserably. 'Yes.'

'And is there?'

'*No.*'

There was several seconds' silence. Melissa was twirling the sugar bowl around the table, avoiding the older girl's eyes. 'Grace, I—you know that there's someone in Athens, someone I was in love with.'

Grace nodded. 'That's about all I know.'

'Demetrius hasn't told you the rest?' Her eyes narrowed suspiciously.

'No, I swear it. He wouldn't gossip about you, even to me.'

'No, I suppose not. Well, this boy, he—he comes from a very poor family and...' She broke off, it was obviously still painful for her.

Grace reached over and covered her hand. 'You don't have to tell me if you don't want to.'

Melissa looked at her belligerently. 'If I don't tell you, will you still help me persuade Demetrius to let me go to Paris?'

'Yes,' Grace said honestly, without hesitation. She wasn't going to force the girl to confide in her. She had hoped to earn that trust.

'Then I'll tell you.' The younger girl smiled, even as her eyes filled with tears. She glanced around to make sure they weren't overheard; the coffee shop was almost deserted. 'I got pregnant. Last summer. In Athens.'

It was all Grace could do not to show how shocked she was. She hadn't expected this.

'It gets worse,' she was warned. 'When I left school, I wanted desperately to visit my home again.

Demetrius took me to Athens for a holiday. We were going to stay the whole summer, he made time especially. I—we'd been there for five weeks when he had to go away. Some emergency had come up, businesswise. We have a maid living in the house, so he didn't worry about my being alone. We also had a gardener, the man who had looked after the grounds since my mother's time there. His son, Nicodemus—Nick, as we called him—was—well, I'd known him when I was a child. Sometimes in the school holidays he came to help his father and—he's very handsome,' she added, looking at Grace almost pleadingly.

Grace nodded. 'And you had a crush on him.'

The response to that was defiant. 'I believed I was in love with him, Grace.'

'I'm sorry. I wasn't being flippant, believe me.'

'It's OK. Well, there I was. I was seventeen, I hadn't had my birthday yet. I—Demetrius didn't know how I felt about Nick, he didn't even know we spent time together, a few hours here and there. I knew he wouldn't approve. Anyway, when he had to leave Athens, I—allowed things to go too far with Nick. We had every opportunity...

'When Demetrius came back I was in a state. He'd been away for two weeks, and during that time I'd missed my period. I couldn't believe it, I was stunned. I couldn't believe I was pregnant. Nick and I, it had only happened twice...'

'Once is enough,' Grace said, thinking aloud. The words echoed inside her head. Once is enough. She kept hearing what she had said, and she squirmed inwardly. It was food for thought, reason for her to think again. 'Go on, Melissa.'

'I didn't tell Demetrius. He guessed. He saw me and Nick in the garden, with our heads together. He was suspicious. I was so panic-stricken, I could hardly put a coherent sentence together. Demetrius confronted me and I broke down, told him. I don't think I need tell you how he reacted. I thought he was going to kill Nick. I was so convinced of it, I got a message to him straight away and told him to hide somewhere for a few days, which he did. Demetrius tried to find out his whereabouts from his father, who didn't know. Nick wisely vanished and told no one where he was going. Demetrius fired his father and brought me back to England immediately.'

Grace's heart had gone out to her. Very quietly she asked, 'And the baby?'

'A short time later, I discovered it was a false alarm. Except that it wasn't. I had conceived, I know I had. My body was different, it had felt different almost immediately.'

Grace sighed. 'And now? How do you feel about Nick now?'

'I hate him!'

'Melissa——'

'It's true. I mean it, Grace. He's a coward, he only wanted one thing and it took me a long time to realise it; I'm so stupid. I wrote to him when I lived in London with Demetrius. I never got an answer. I assumed my letters hadn't got to him, I suspected his father had intercepted them, but in fact that wasn't the case. Demetrius didn't know about this, of course. Then a few months ago I phoned the house in Athens and eventually—after several calls—I got the maid to take a message to Nick. His family hasn't got a telephone. The maid was difficult to persuade, you can imagine. Eventually she got Nick to the house and I talked to him ... '

'And?'

'And he didn't want to know. He told me in precisely those words. He'd had my letters and ignored them. He told me to stop pestering him.' She shrugged, bravely, but it was hurting. 'So that's the end of that, and you'll believe there is no danger of my sneaking off to Greece. I'm trying very hard not to feel bitter, but—as I sit here now I feel that I hate Nick.'

Grace caught hold of her hand again. 'Believe it or not, it will wear off. All of it. You can take my word on that. Thank you for confiding in me. I'm—I feel honoured, really I do. You've got to put it behind you now, all of it. You're very young and you have a good future ahead of you.'

'I hope so.' Melissa looked at her, with that hope. 'You'll help me persuade Demetrius to let me have my passport, go to Paris?'

'I will.' Grace did not anticipate any difficulty in that. She was, at that moment, more concerned with her own problem. Demetrius' problem. Their problem.

By the time she got home that evening, Grace was exhausted, emotionally and physically. Her mind had been whirring all day. When the phone rang just half an hour after she'd got in she was inclined to ignore it, to let Matty answer it and say she wasn't home. Only the prospect of it being Demetrius made her pick it up.

It was her father again. When he'd said that morning that he would talk to her later, she had assumed he meant later in the week. He was still

on cloud nine by the sound of it. Again, Grace had
to psyche herself into reacting appropriately when
she heard what he'd been up to. He and Phyllis.

'You'll be pleased to hear I'm coming home this
weekend.'

She wasn't, it meant that privacy with Demetrius
would be impossible in either house. But maybe that
was a good thing? Not that she had been thinking
of... she wasn't at all sure *what* she was thinking
of doing now, since that shocking conversation with
Melissa.

'I'm delighted to hear it, Daddy. I can take it
Phyllis will be with you?'

'Naturally. We're going to have a party on
Saturday night.'

'A party? At the manor?'

'Aha! I thought that would please you! We're
going to celebrate. They're all coming to the manor
this weekend, so go out and buy yourself a new
dress. My treat.'

'All?' This weekend? It was more than enough
to depress her, coming on top of everything else.
What lousy timing! Of all the weekends to choose...
But what could she say?

'Phyllis' family, all of them. She's just phoned
me to say her son can make it, Saturday to Sunday
at least. I expect she's talking to her daughter right
now, she couldn't reach her earlier, but she thinks
it'll be all right. It's the Bank Holiday, remember?'

Grace hadn't remembered. 'So we'll all have
Monday off,' her father went on. 'I got hold of
Thomas at lunch time, he can make it, too. And
there'll be Demetrius and Melissa, of course. We're
just having people who are close to us.'

People who are close to us. Among whom Melissa and Demetrius were included. But . . . she could no longer be sure she had any kind of relationship with Demetrius, not now. She managed to put a smile in her voice. 'It sounds lovely.'

'I'm about to ring Desmond and Belle Wakeham, I think we should invite them, don't you?'

'Yes, I do. Do you want me to plan it with Matty?'

'I'd like to talk to her myself, she doesn't know what the party's in aid of yet! It will come as quite a shock to her, won't it?'

Grace's smile was a real one then. Just what planet did her father live on? 'No, Daddy, it won't. People have eyes, you know. Even Matty. *Especially* Matty. I'll fetch her to the phone. Oh— er—what time will everyone be arriving?'

'Various. Phyllis and I will get there mid-afternoon, on Friday. I don't know about Sally, her daughter, yet. Thomas will be driving down on Saturday morning, he said. He's going to contact Sally and offer her a lift. Phyllis' son and family will be the last to arrive, Saturday afternoon. Unfortunately, he'll have to leave first thing Sunday morning because he's on call for part of the holiday weekend. That's as much as I can tell you.'

It was enough. Grace's heart was heavy; she was in no mood for a party, but there was no way in the world she would let her father and Phyllis know it. Or anyone else. She would just have to wait for an opportunity to talk to Demetrius—or rather, to listen to him.

What *did* he have to say to her? Was he simply going to finish with her or was he going to talk about where they were heading in their relationship? Or rather, where they weren't heading? Where they weren't heading...a dozen times that day, she had recounted the conversation with Melissa. Her shock had been well concealed in front of the girl but—*pregnant*? How awful for her! Just thinking of Demetrius' reaction to that made Grace shudder.

Going to bed that night, she was as agitated as she had been the previous night. It had been a long twenty-four hours. So much had happened. Realising she loved Demetrius had brought an immeasurable calm, but it had been short-lived. Very. As for his reaction to her offer—she was at a loss to understand his anger with her. He hadn't phoned this evening, she wondered whether he would ring from Scotland. Oh, what wouldn't she give to know what was going through his mind?

CHAPTER TEN

As TIME passed, infuriatingly slowly, Grace became more and more distracted, more and more nervous. Demetrius phoned her at home on Tuesday morning, which was the day her business was closed, but it was a brief call because he was due in a meeting at any minute. All he asked was whether she was all right, Melissa likewise. Not wishing to detain him, she told him quickly about her father's engagement to Phyllis Radcliffe, and mentioned the party on Saturday. 'They want to celebrate, naturally. He's over the moon by the sound of him.'

'I'll look forward to it. That's the nicest news I've had for days. I have to go now, Grace. Take care.' And then he was gone.

After putting down the phone, she rang Melissa. 'Demetrius just rang, he was in a big hurry and asked me to say hello. How are you?'

'OK. I hope he gets back quickly, I can't stand the suspense.'

She couldn't stand it? If only she knew how Grace was feeling! 'Don't worry about it. It'll be fine.' She went on to tell her about Saturday's party, her father's engagement to Phyllis. There wasn't much reaction from her, which was understandable. Her mind was elsewhere. In Paris, for example. Her reaction was merely polite.

'How lovely for them. I'll be there, of course I will.' There was a momentary pause before she had her brainwave. 'Hey, it's your day off, why don't we go in to Reading, go shopping?'

Grace jumped at the suggestion. 'Better still, why don't we go into London? We can spend the day there, find something nice for the party, and maybe a few other things! I'll pick you up in fifteen minutes.'

They drove as far as South Ealing, parked the car and took the Tube into the West End.

The sun was shining, the shops were crowded and everywhere one turned, foreign voices could be heard. The tourists were there in their thousands. Still, it was good for the economy.

'What do you think of this?'

Grace gave up. They were in a boutique off Oxford Street, and it was the tenth time Melissa had asked the question, holding against her some garment or other. This time it was a deep purple dress with yellow dots on it.

'They'll see you coming in that. Don't ask me. Our taste in clothes is different, to say the least!'

'You're not being very helpful,' Melissa complained. 'I'll try it on, then give me your opinion. I have to get a few things together, I'm very short of summer clothes.'

They had a late lunch; by the time they got back to the car in Ealing they were shattered, hot and sticky and loaded with shopping bags. 'You realise,' Melissa said, 'that if Demetrius doesn't say yes to Paris, today will have been a waste of time. I'll be a hermit again and won't need new clothes. In fact, I shall probably kill myself.'

'Oh, that's even better,' Grace teased, 'then you won't need any clothes at all.'

'Thank you very much!'

It had been fun spending the day with Melissa; the energy and enthusiasm she had shown had been contagious. Grace was going to miss her when she went to Paris. She was pleased for her, but she would miss her, for she had grown to love her.

Neither of them had spoken to Demetrius by the time Wednesday evening rolled around. Grace had Melissa round to dinner in the evening and it was the first question she asked when she arrived.

'Have you heard from Demetrius?'

The teenager grinned. 'You've got it bad, haven't you?'

Horrified, Grace denied it. The thought that her true feelings for Demetrius were showing panicked her. She didn't want anyone to realise how deeply she was in love with him, Melissa or anyone else. And most especially Demetrius himself. 'Don't be so dramatic, that's typical of you. Naturally I'm fond of your brother, I just want to know he's all right, that's all.'

'Is that a fact? Sorry, the answer's no. He hasn't phoned me today, which is odd.'

'Precisely my point. He had left a message on the answering machine at work this morning—at God knows what time. I was there at ten past eight.'

'And what did he say?'

Grace shrugged, there wasn't much to tell. What little there was, she didn't mind saying. 'Just hello, sorry I'm talking to your machine. I wanted to tell you I will be back on Friday.' No sooner had she relayed the message than the phone rang.

'That's probably him now,' Melissa said, but Grace was already on her way to the hall to answer it. It *was* Demetrius.

'Is Melissa with you? She's not answering the phone.'

Grace sat down by the telephone table, disappointed by his businesslike attitude. 'Yes, we're just about to eat.'

'Ah. So she's in good hands. Has she given you any problems?'

'Not at all. We spent the day in London doing some shopping yesterday and we really enjoyed it. I enjoyed her company, to be more accurate.'

He grunted. 'I'm sorry, Grace, but I have to dash off again. I'm still trouble-shooting.'

'Is that what you're doing?'

'That, and some tricky negotiations. They should be concluded over lunch tomorrow. You got my message this morning? Saying I'd be back on Friday?'

'Yes. I—what sort of time?'

'As soon as I can. Probably late afternoon.'

'Demetrius, I—it's going to be very difficult this weekend, we're going to have a house full of people. The party, you know.' She went on to explain who was coming, and when. When she'd finished, he grunted again.

'I have to go, I've got a dinner engagement, so listen because I'm only going to say this once. You'll make time, organise it. I told you I want to talk to you and I'm not prepared to wait. I intend to talk to you on Friday night, so detach yourself from your company.'

Grace was about to protest, but there was little point. It would only annoy him and he was in a hurry. 'Give my love to my sister,' he said hastily, and hung up.

'It was Demetrius, he sends his love.' She walked back into the drawing-room despondently.

'Why didn't he ask to talk to me?' Melissa was indignant. 'Is something wrong?'

'No, no, he was going off to have dinner with someone, business people, I suppose.'

'What's the matter? You're not worrying in case he's going out with a woman, are you?'

'No.' The word came strongly enough but— maybe he was? If he was going to finish with her, what was there to stop him?

They were in the middle of dinner when Melissa remarked on how quiet Grace was, how nervy. She made the excuse of feeling tired, hoping it would convince the younger girl, feeling grateful when she said she wouldn't stay too late. Grace ran her home at nine-thirty, checked that all was OK in the house and went straight back to the manor, to bed.

She wasn't tired, she was keyed up. She told herself she needed to think, but hadn't she done enough of that? It wasn't getting her anywhere, she was just winding herself up more, thinking, worrying. As for Friday night, she could detach herself from her father and Phyllis, of course, though her father would think it odd in view of her recent protests when he hadn't come home for the weekend. She would explain that she had to be over at the Knights' house because there was something very important they had to discuss. Which was, after all, the truth.

It was Melissa she was thinking of. There was no way that particular discussion could take precedence over her talking privately with Demetrius. Melissa was almost as wound up as Grace, and she wasn't trying to hide it. 'You'll come round on

Friday, won't you?' she'd said earlier. 'As soon as you can get away. We'll talk to Demetrius then. I'll make him one of his favourite meals, get him in a good mood——'

'Melissa, I...I need to talk to him myself.'

That piece of information had been completely misunderstood. Melissa had shaken her head firmly. 'No, I don't expect you to do it *for* me, I just want you to support me. We'll all talk.'

It rained on Thursday. It rained solidly all morning. Grace woke up at five o'clock with the intention of going for a ride—an idea she abandoned when she saw the weather, even though Annabel was in need of some exercise. With Demetrius away there had been no incentive, somehow, to get up and make the effort.

There was no word from him that day. The next she heard from him was late Friday afternoon, when he called her from home. 'I'm back,' he said without preamble. 'And my sister tells me there's something "absolutely *desperate*" she wants to talk about.' He sounded weary but vaguely amused. 'She informs me also that you're coming over here tonight, that she can't tell me what it is until you're here. So what's going on?'

'I'll come over at nine, after dinner. Daddy and Phyllis got here about ten minutes ago and I feel I really must spend a bit of time with them.'

'Which is a non-answer if ever I heard one.'

'Demetrius, please bear with me. I'll see you at nine.' She hung up before he could say anything else. Silently she said, I love you. I love you and I'm scared.

*   *   *

Seeing him again came as a shock to her. She had dressed carefully, had made up subtly, put on the perfume he'd admired countless times and had driven round in a state of nervous anxiety so acute she felt she would never be normal again.

Her heart plummeted when she saw him. He and Melissa were in the kitchen, tidying up. Demetrius was just setting the dishwasher going when Grace let herself in the back door, and he straightened, his eyes narrowing slightly as she walked in. He seemed to be looking at her suspiciously, probing her eyes intently, and she couldn't understand why. He did not appear to experience any pleasure in seeing her.

She, on the other hand, felt her heart leap painfully in her breast. It was all she could do to stop herself running to him, her desire to throw her arms around him was almost irresistible. He was wearing trousers and a white shirt, unbuttoned at the neck, the sleeves rolled up. Her eyes took in everything about him swiftly, the hard muscles of his forearms, the tanned column of his throat, the place where the hair on his chest was visible. And his face, beloved, strong, handsome, so very familiar to her in all its details, all its moods... yet it felt as though she hadn't set eyes on that face for years.

It wasn't easy to make her greeting casual, but somehow she managed. 'Hi, how was your trip?'

He was still looking at her oddly. 'Fine. Tiring but successful, thanks. So,' he added, turning to his sister, smiling finally, 'since you insisted on changing my plans tonight, both of you, let's make ourselves comfortable in the sitting-room and discuss this world-shattering event, whatever it is.'

It took some time. Actually, the response Melissa had hoped for took only a few minutes; not only was Demetrius in agreement with her plans, he was obviously genuinely pleased and as co-operative as he could be. There was only one awkward moment, right at the start, as soon as she mentioned that the course was in Paris.

'Paris?' Demetrius stiffened slightly, his eyes scanning those of his sister, not unlike the way they had scanned Grace's when she had first arrived. They were full of questions.

Grace spoke up quickly. 'Melissa, I think that what you have to tell Demetrius straight away is that you're completely over... you know. Reassure him you're not going to run off to Athens when he hands your passport over.'

Melissa did just that. It was all as easy as Grace had expected it to be. The teenager was joyous, she could hardly contain her excitement. She couldn't seem to stop talking, even after everything had been settled, after she had shown her brother the letters from France: from the academy, from Marianne and her family.

Grace kept glancing at her watch, very surreptitiously. She could hardly tell Melissa to shut up, to keep her excitement to herself, but it was almost half-past eleven before she said she was going to bed, before she finally left Grace and Demetrius alone.

The atmosphere in the room changed instantly, suddenly the two of them were like strangers. Neither of them seemed to have anything to say. Demetrius got up, poured himself another drink and asked if she would like a refill.

'No, I—no, thanks.'

The door opened. Melissa was back. 'Demetrius, you are agreeable to my leaving in July, aren't you? I mean, that'll give me a chance——'

'To see something of Paris while Marianne's on holiday. Yes, Melissa. You did mention it earlier.'

'But you didn't say yes.'

'Yes. Yes, yes, yes,' he smiled. 'Anything you like!'

She gave a whoop and disappeared again.

Grace was glad of her reappearance, it had broken the tension. 'She's a good girl, Demetrius. I'm sure she'll make a go of this. It will be the sort of career that will enable her to work anywhere in the world, if she wants to.'

'I've no doubt she will. I think she'll make a go of it, she's certainly keen. I don't remember her being so enthusiastic about anything before—except that boy. I gather she told you all about that? Everything?'

'Everything.' His face had changed, had grown taut. Feeling obliged to say something further, Grace added, 'It's over, Demetrius. She was seventeen and she made a mistake. We all make them. You have to forgive her.'

'I forgave her long since.' He was still leaning on the bar, making no attempt to get closer to her. 'I just don't want her to make the same mistake again.'

'She's hardly likely to do that, it was a hard lesson.'

'I know, I think you're right. That's why I have no qualms about letting her loose in Paris.'

He paused, and silence hung in the air for seconds. Grace filled it by apologising; she could sense his frustration, she had been aware of it all along. 'I'm sorry about tonight, I couldn't very well——'

'No. I know. Forget it.' He looked at his watch. 'You don't have to dash off, do you?'

She should have said yes, but she didn't. She had to be up early to give Matty a hand tomorrow, and Thomas would be arriving with Sally Radcliffe in the morning, she wasn't sure what time. He was giving her a lift down from Cambridge.

But she didn't have a chance to answer Demetrius one way or another. It was hopeless, Melissa was back. Again. This time she didn't merely pop her head round the door, she came in. It obviously hadn't occurred to her it might be inappropriate. 'Demetrius, we didn't talk about money. I mean my keep and everything. We discussed everything else except——'

His patience ran out. 'Tomorrow,' he said firmly. 'We'll discuss it *tomorrow*. Now scoot, Melissa. And do *not* interrupt us again, please.'

'Oh!' Her eyes went straight to Grace, an apology in them. She mouthed the words and retreated rapidly.

Grace watched as Demetrius downed the drink he'd poured. She got to her feet. 'I'd better go, it is late.'

'No!' He moved, quickly, to where she was standing. 'I—I've been doing a lot of thinking since we were last together.'

'You mean since we fought.'

'Fought? Yes, I suppose that's what it was. You said some pretty outrageous things, Grace.'

She stiffened inwardly. 'You were pretty outrageous yourself.'

'I meant, what I meant was—dammit, I've got so much to say to you, I don't know where to begin.'

She sighed. 'Well...I've got to be up early tomorrow and it's turned midnight.'

'Wait!' He reached for her, his hands clamping firmly on her shoulders. It was by no means a delicate touch, but it got to her just the same. His touch, any kind of touch, was enough to make her pulses go into overdrive. 'Just a minute, please. Grace, I—I had no idea, you realise that, don't you?'

'About what?'

'You, your lack of experience, as you put it.' He looked troubled, apologetic. In turn, it made her feel silly, but he was determined to say what he wanted to say. 'I had assumed...assumed otherwise. You appear to be so sophisticated, so—hey, there's no need to blush! I was touched, I am touched. It made me feel...I don't know how to explain it. I've been blaming myself all week, I kept thinking about what happened to Melissa in Athens and——'

'That's ridiculous.' She shrugged his hands from her shoulders, stepping away from him. If he kept his hands on her she wouldn't be able to think properly. 'Melissa was seventeen and I'm twenty-four. You never took advantage, I know how your mind's been working, but you can't compare me with your sister. I am by no means an innocent.'

'But you are,' he said softly, smiling.

She looked away, her blush deepening. 'I think it's laughable.'

Very quietly, he said, 'I don't.' He saw her eyes move to the door. 'It's all right, Melissa won't come in here again, it's more than she dare do.'

'I know.'

'So why the anxiety? You want to run away, is that it? Are you afraid of me, Grace?'

'Of course not.' It was just that she wished he would get it over with. 'Why don't you just say it, Demetrius? You've discovered I'm not your kind of woman, so that's it. We're finished.'

'Finished?' He looked as though she had slapped him. '*Finished?* Grace, I love you!' He said it again, very quietly this time. 'Not only are you very much my kind of woman, not only do I want you, I happen to *love* you.'

She could do no more than stare at him, hoping against hope that he was sincere, that he really meant what he had said.

'Tell me,' he urged, 'tell me what you're thinking and feeling. I want to hear you say the words.'

She couldn't. This—all of it—it was too much to hope for, it couldn't be real. 'I—want you, too.' It was all she could manage.

Demetrius smiled without humour. 'No, not that. I know that. What else, my darling? What else do you feel for me?'

Gripped by an irrational panic, she turned her head away. Did he mean what he'd said? *Did* he? If only she could be sure of him . . .

He caught hold of her, his hand cupping her chin, forcing her to look at him. 'I'm not talking about desire. If you were out specifically to seduce me tonight, you'd fail.'

Her laughter was nervous, wobbly. 'I don't believe that.'

Demetrius laughed, too. 'I can understand that. But it's become a matter of principle,' he added, serious again. 'You've accused me of lying to you, of inveigling, and my principles, my pride, don't take very kindly to that.'

'That—that's honest of you.'

'I've always been honest with you,' he said softly. He still had hold of her, gently, at arm's length. 'Isn't it high time you were honest with me? Tell me, *tell me* what it is you're thinking, feeling.'

There was, she knew, no point in holding back any longer. He already knew. 'I love you,' she said on a sigh. 'I love you, Demetrius.'

He gathered her into his arms, he kissed her long and hard—yet there was a certain tenderness about it, too. It was a kiss unlike any they had shared before. Grace believed it was she who was making it somehow different. All that she felt for him was expressed in the way she kissed him in return: love, tenderness, respect, desire, everything. It seemed as if an eternity had passed since she was last in his arms.

Reluctantly he raised his head, his mouth against her temple. 'That's what I wanted to hear, there's a good girl! It's a relief, isn't it, being able to say it finally? Oh, Grace, you don't know how desperately I've wanted to hear you say those words!'

'You—you knew? When did you know?'

'I haven't known for long. I had to think things through and work it out for myself. All this time I've...been hoping. I've waited and waited for you to give yourself to me. At first I wanted it to be simply because you wanted it, too, with your mind as well as your body, but as time passed I wanted more than that from you. Don't you see, I kept my hands off you as best I could *because* I loved you. I wanted you to love me as I love you.'

Grace stiffened in his arms. He held her tighter, so tightly she could hardly breathe. But she couldn't get enough of it. She didn't want him ever to let her go.

'I mean it, Grace. I've loved you for a long time. I thought—you gave no sign of how you really felt about me. On the contrary. It was only after you made your offer on the phone earlier this week that I realised. That, after you'd told me I would be the first. I can't tell you how much I loved you for that, how much it meant to me.'

'But—you were angry with me!'

'Briefly, very briefly, my darling. And only because I knew how your mind was working, that you assumed the continuation of our relationship hinged on sex. It didn't make me feel good, I can tell you. But as soon as I put the phone down and thought about it, I understood. I knew it could mean only one thing.'

'Quite the detective, aren't you?' She wriggled away from him a little so she could look at him. 'And now? As you once asked me, what happens next?'

Demetrius took both her hands in his and led her to the settee. He was laughing. 'Sit down and I'll tell you. We get married, of course.' He laughed again when he saw the look of shock on her face. 'Dear God, you really have had your doubts, haven't you? You didn't believe me when I told you I love you, and you still don't! Grace Allinson, what do I have to do, put it in writing?'

'But——'

'But nothing. There are no buts. I love you and I want to marry you just as quickly as it can be arranged.'

'Demetrius, you—you're not the marrying kind.'

He seemed taken aback. 'Who says?'

'You. Melissa. Me. Everyone.'

'What nonsense! I've never actually said that, and what would Melissa know? She doesn't know how I feel about you, not the full extent of it, anyway.'

'But—but you're thirty-six years old.'

'What on earth has that got to do with anything?' He was serious again, very. 'Are you worrying about our age difference, is that it?'

'No, you idiot. I mean—all these years, you've escaped from marriage.'

'Escaped? My darling, don't you understand? Still? Oh, I've loved before, sort of. Briefly. But never like this, I've never felt about anyone the way I feel about you. With you it's everything, Grace, it's *everything*. I can't settle for less than marriage with you. I want to bring up a family with you, I want to spend the rest of my life with you, every hour of every day with you, every night...' He grinned, sliding his arms around her. 'Especially every night.'

'Demetrius, you really are incorrigible!' She held him away, a half-hearted effort. 'Why didn't you say any of this before, when you made what I thought was a stupid and insincere proposal, last Sunday?'

'You didn't give me the chance.' He shrugged, realising his answer wasn't good enough. 'Think about it, about the circumstances. I was—wound up to say the least. I wasn't thinking straight, you were screaming at me. I was talking off the top of my head and yet I meant it. Grace, all I've been waiting for was a sign from you that you felt the

same way. I would have married you weeks ago.'
He paused, sighing. 'Well, to be practical, there was
also the problem of Melissa.'

'What problem?'

'You know what I mean, my darling. I couldn't
have expected you to live with her, to start married
life with my crazy sister in the same house. It
wouldn't have been fair to you, I wouldn't have
expected it of you.'

'I love Melissa,' Grace said honestly. 'I really do.
Though I have to admit,' she added, because it was
the truth, 'I wouldn't relish the idea of living with
her!'

'Well, that particular problem has been solved
for us, for the next two years at least. Knowing her,
she'll come back from Paris married or something.'
He smiled, reaching for her again. His kiss was
familiar in its hunger this time, as his mouth moved
against hers, as she invited his exploration, and they
drank deeply of one another, embracing tightly,
unable to get close enough. But, again, Demetrius
called a halt.

'Demetrius, for heaven's sake, stop teasing me!'

He didn't, he kissed her again and again, holding
her at bay once more when she was so far gone that
she couldn't think straight. 'Ah, but revenge is
sweet!'

'Demetrius——'

'Control yourself, woman!'

She didn't, she slid her hand along his thigh.
'But, darling, what about our...unfinished business?'

He looked heavenward. 'Precisely. You haven't
said you'll marry me yet.'

Grace hooted at that. 'What is this, blackmail?'

'If that's how you want to see it. So?'

'Marry you? I'll do anything to get my hands on your body!'

'You're a wicked, wicked woman, Grace Allinson, and I love you. Now keep your distance,' he added, grinning. 'You're a drug to me, and I am totally and completely hooked. Do you think they'll still be up, at the manor?'

'What time is it?'

Unbelievably, it was a quarter to three.

'A quarter to three!' Grace was horrified. 'I hope nobody's waited up for me!'

'What's the problem?'

'They'll be worried, they'll be demented!'

'Why, when you're with me?'

'That's why!' she laughed.

He tickled her, running his hands over her ribs until she was helpless. She collapsed against him, begging him to stop. 'Please, darling, stop that!'

'Then say it and say it properly this time. Say you'll marry me before Melissa goes away.'

She sobered. Yes, it would have to be before Melissa went to Paris in July, she would simply have to be at their wedding. She would miss Sir Nigel's marriage to Phyllis, but she wasn't going to miss her brother's wedding.

'I'll marry you, Demetrius, just as quickly as I can.' Grace smiled; it looked as if she was going to be a June bride. 'Indeed,' she added, thinking aloud, 'it looks as though I'm going to beat my father to the altar!' She was thinking about her father, wondering how much of a surprise this would be to him. To anyone. It seemed that she was the most surprised of all, now she came to think about it.

'Since Nigel isn't getting married till the end of August, the answer to that is yes, you are, and we'll be away for several weeks on a long, long honeymoon. We'll come back a few days before his wedding. When are we going to tell him?'

'Tomorrow night, when we're celebrating his engagement to Phyllis.'

'Right, that's when we'll announce ours—and in the morning we'll go shopping for a ring. You don't think they'll mind our stealing a little of their limelight?'

Grace closed her eyes, there were tears in them because she was so indescribably happy. 'No,' she said softly. 'I don't think they'll mind in the least...'

 **Harlequin Romance**

Coming Next Month

2941 WHIRLPOOL OF PASSION Emma Darcy
Ashley finds Cairo fascinating, and even more so the mysterious sheikh she encounters in the casino. She's aware their attraction is mutual, but doesn't take it seriously until he kidnaps her....

2942 THIS TIME ROUND Catherine George
It's all very well for Leo Seymour to want to share her life, Davina thinks, but she can't forget that his first love married her brother years ago. Would Davina's secret love for him be enough to sustain their relationship?

2943 TO TAME A TYCOON Emma Goldrick
It isn't that Laura absolutely doesn't trust tycoon Robert Carlton; she only wants to protect her young daughter from him. And Robert has all his facts wrong about Laura. If there was only some way to change their minds about each other.

2944 AT FIRST SIGHT Eva Rutland
From the time designer Cicely Roberts accidentally meets psychiatrist-author Mark Dolan, her life is turned upside down. Even problems she didn't know she had get straightened out—and love comes to Cicely at last!

2945 CATCH A DREAM Celia Scott
Jess is used to rescuing her hapless cousin Kitty from trouble, but confronting Andros Kalimantis in his lonely tower in Greece is the toughest thing she's ever done. And Kitty hadn't warned her that Andros is a millionaire....

2946 A NOT-SO-PERFECT MARRIAGE Edwina Shore
James's suspected unfaithfulness was the last straw. So Roz turned to photography, left James to his business and made a successful career on her own. So why should she even consider letting him back into her life now?

Available in November wherever paperback books are sold, or through Harlequin Reader Service:

In the U.S.
901 Fuhrmann Blvd.
P.O. Box 1397
Buffalo, N.Y. 14240-1397

In Canada
P.O. Box 603
Fort Erie, Ontario
L2A 5X3

Take 4 best-selling love stories FREE
Plus get a FREE surprise gift!

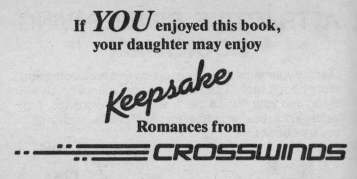